THE
CELLAR

A CIVIL WAR NOVELLA BY

C. G. RICHARDSON
8/6/2013

Dedicated to David "Shorty" Rawls,

Though long gone your memory keeps me company.

Foreward

This is a work of historic fiction. The characters and specific events are purely from my imagination, but the background events are as close to what was going on in the 1860s as I can make them. Sherman's army was indeed foraging in Northern Mississippi in 1863, well before the march to the sea. Some minor incidents related were from memoirs written by men in my Great Grandfather's unit, the 40th Illinois Volunteer Infantry. The clumsy butchering of the cow by the roadside, the improvised rolls, and the slave children bringing water to the troops all came from a couple of fellows I feel like I know personally from having read their recollections again and again. I became acquainted with E. J. Hart and John T. Hunt while I was doing research for my previous Novel, "Sergeant Tom's War". I feel I owe them a debt for leaving some intimation of what life was like for my Great Granddad and Great Uncles as they made their way through the conflagration.

Table of Contents

Chapter 1 – The Sins of the Father

Ike woke up to darkness and silence. Blinking a couple of times didn't seem to make any difference, there was as much light visible with his eyelids closed as with them open. Turning his head from side to side only revealed that he was stiff from having lain in the same position for too long. For a few moments he imagined that he might be dead. An inventory of his numerous hurts erased all doubt and convinced him that he was still among the living.

An indistinct sound, like someone calling his name, startled Ike. His reflexive jerking brought more pain. The voice sounded as if it came from the bottom of a well. He strained to try to identify where the voice and the snatch of laughter that followed it might have come from but heard nothing save the sound of his own heartbeat in his ears and the ringing noises that had been near constant since the night of the artillery barrage back at Pittsburgh landing.

Ike's leg ached in a way that convinced him that it was broken. It had been immobilized with a pair of wooden splints. He felt light headed and weak as if he had been suffering from a long illness. There was a cloth tied snugly around the top of his head. A two fingered exploration of the area covered by the cloth was rewarded with a stabbing pain just above his left eye. The spot seemed moist and there was a small indentation which stung when pressure was applied.

Where ever he was felt cool but not uncomfortably so. He didn't feel as sick to his stomach as he had been back, back where? He tried unsuccessfully to remember where he had been the last time he was conscious. How long ago had it been? He was laying on something soft but not too soft. He carefully patted his surroundings with hands that he couldn't see. The soft blanket underneath him was spread over a pile of straw strewn on a hard floor. He raised his right arm slowly over his head and moved it about to see if there was anything above him. His left arm encountered the cool surface of a stone wall about a foot from his shoulder. He couldn't shake the feeling that he might be in a coffin or at least a tomb. Finding no lid above his head to stop him, he attempted to sit up.

Everything seemed to spin and float when Ike tried raising himself up. As dark as it was, colors bloomed before his eyes and he felt like he was floating. A couple of seconds after his attempt to sit up he was flat on his back again. He heard the laughter again just before he lost consciousness. He slept and dreamed of home.

Emma was sitting on the porch, mending a pair of his old trousers. She shook her head at how hard he was on his clothes, but she smiled and made her careful stitches count as she extended the life of Ike's pants. Their bulldog Freddy was lying at Emma's feet with his massive head on his paws. Ike wanted to take his beautiful wife in his arms and kiss her passionately but he couldn't move in that direction. Freddy looked up as if he had spotted an intruder but then the whole scene floated backwards and disappeared.

A wall of flame appeared, searing his exposed skin and making his clothing smoke. He could barely keep his eyes open against the glare, but he was looking for something or someone in the conflagration. Ike thought once more that he was dead and that the sermons on Hell were more than just allegory to frighten the guilty to repentance. He could feel his skin blister but he couldn't seem to back away from the fire as he desperately searched. He was confused about what or who he was looking for. Just when he thought he would explode from the heat oblivion took him once more. Dreamless sleep overcame him for a while, giving his mind a rest from its inventory of a jumble of tangled memories.

A more recent and somehow more important scene swam before him and solidified. Ike was with his squad on a foraging detail. They had come upon an unusually prosperous looking farmhouse with a chicken coop and a pen that held the first hogs they had seen in weeks. Johnny O'Donnell joked about pork chops for supper as a middle aged woman came out on the porch and glared at the blue coated men standing in her yard. The woman was attractive and would have been more so had it not been for the look of disdain as she swept the men with her gaze. The sun beat down on them fiercely and the look from her eyes seemed to add to the waves of heat that were making Ike feel queasy already. Ike had been feverish all morning and the heat was adding to his woes. If he hadn't been so hungry he probably would have went on sick call and stayed back in camp, but the possibility of finding something to eat enticed him to go on this little adventure. He had seen the water pump and trough by the barn and quietly made his way toward it in hopes of quenching his thirst and cooling his throbbing head. The weary soldier had leaned his rifle against the watering trough and scooped water into his hands and began to splash his face.

Sarge had tipped his hat to the woman who stood with her arms crossed studying them as if they were something that had been accidentally tracked into her parlor on the sole of someone's shoe. He had informed her that the Union army was in need of supplies and would be confiscating some of the hogs and chickens. Sarge sounded like a defeated man as the woman ignored his speech and turned to go back into her house.

Sarge often said that he hated "Jay hawking" detail worse than facing artillery. He had told Ike that it made him feel like the lowest kind of thief to take food from civilians, even the rabid secessionists of northern Mississippi. Sarge had stood there speechless, with his head down and his hat in his hand as the woman walked back through her door, glancing over her shoulder at the woods. That was when all hell broke loose in the yard.

Rifles popped in the trees that edged the clearing. Ike heard the too familiar buzzing of the minie' balls as they flew and the splatting noise of the big lead slugs burrowing into the flesh of men he had shared so much with over the last two years. A bullet grazed his forehead and set it on fire as he dove over the watering trough for cover. He seemed to be hanging in mid air when the bullet hit him. When the impact came his suspension ceased and he felt like he was plummeting from a great height. He felt the bone in his left leg crack as he went down hard and hit it on a rock. He could hear screaming and moaning from the other side of the yard as another round bored all the way through the trough just at the water level letting loose a brief stream of cool water that jetted to the dusty ground just in front of Ike's face. He felt dust and then thin mud splattering in his face and then once again there was nothing.

The wounded soldier's brain had been traumatized by the blow that had hammered in a small portion of its protective skull. Ike neared the threshold of death and fought back several times as his brain fired millions of messages here and there. Instructions went out to vital organs, memories were processed, and some were lost or misplaced as parts of his mind shut down in order to maintain his vital functions. His subconscious dealt with the approach of possible death by replaying images of his life. For a few moments it was taken somewhere beyond the barnyard where his physical body lay fighting for its continued existence.

For a short interval peace reigned as Ike stood on the bank of a creek. The creek crossed a meadow that was in full bloom of a perfect spring. The clearest water he had ever seen babbled across rocks in the creek and made a chuckling noise. Ike wanted to take off his shoes and feel the coolness of the water as he waded across. In the distance a figure stood on the edge of a green wood. Ike wanted to go to this figure and was about to step off into the water when he was drawn back into darkness.

After a brief interlude of near consciousness and searing pain Ike's mind went back to Pittsburg landing and the bloody April morning that had taken his brother and so many of his friends from Company D. They had finally "seen the elephant" and the beast's rampage had stomped them flat as they made their first contact with the enemy. Ike seemed to be marching endlessly across overgrown fields littered with corpses in blue and gray uniforms. As he strode through the carnage young voices in his head were repeating Tennyson's "Charge of the Light Brigade"

> Half a league, half a league,
> Half a league onward.
> All in the valley of death
> Rode the six hundred.

Came the sound of school children repeating the poem they had memorized as Ike marched across what looked to be the valley of death. The voices sounded young and innocent and Ike smiled with pride at how well they repeated the lines.

Storm'd at with shot and shell,
Boldly they rode and well,
Into the jaws of Death,
Into the mouth of Hell...

A small boy's voice was heard giggling at the word "hell" and the children all broke into embarrassed laughter. Ike continued marching, unhappy with the interruption.

Scenes from the two days of wholesale killing of fellow human beings, losing friends, and living in terror beyond anything he could have imagined floated in front of him. He found himself standing in line among those who were left in his squad after the first day's carnage and who had spent the miserable night in a pouring rain as they waited to do it all over again the next day.

He could see the rain running in a steady stream off Sarge's hat when one of the big artillery shells from the gunboats arced overhead and lit up the sky for a few moments before it began to descend and wreak havoc with the enemy scattered to their front. It might have been a funny sight under other circumstances than these, but the look on the face of the man under the streaming hat was so full of anguish that he wanted to reach out to him. Ike had lost a brother in the fight and his Sergeant had lost a son. He tried to put his hands out toward the man but the image floated away into darkness.

They were digging, digging in mud while they scraped out the long trench for the Rebels. The dead men laying there seemed like an embarrassment to him; their presence was an accusation against him and his comrades and he wanted to get them under the ground as quick as he could so he wouldn't have to look at them anymore. It felt like sweeping dirt under a rug to hide it, when you were supposed to be cleaning the house. He dug frantically until the blisters on his hands bled. The irrational idea had come to Ike that if they could just get the hole filled and covered before God looked this direction and noticed about 700 dead men lying about things would be alright and he worked feverishly to that end. In his dream a bloated corpse that he and Johnny O'Donnell dragged to the edge of the hole opened its gummy eyes and leered at Ike. "You killed me, blue belly and now you'll pay!"

Ike woke up screaming at the sound of the corpse's voice as it grated its accusation at him and blew the stench of its decay into his face. The sound of his scream was swallowed by the darkness that still surrounded him. He laid panting and sweating in the dark. His body was drenched in sweat and in a way that felt like he might have had a fever and it had just broken. He lay there for a while trying to discern where he was but it was still a mystery.

"You must have had a terrible dream young man." a female voice droned from the gloom. Ike almost screamed again. He tensed and his breath caught in his throat until he nearly passed out. Finally his body relaxed and he regained enough lucidity to respond.

"Who...... Who's there?"

There was a scratching, then a snap and a hiss as the smell of sulphur assaulted his nose. A face appeared above him, painted yellow by the light of a match. Ike recognized the face of the woman on the porch that had turned her back on Sarge before.......... "Oh God!" Ike thought, "Sarge and my squad.....are they all dead?"

The woman used the match to light an oil lamp that had been sitting on a small table next to a kitchen chair. He surmised that she must have been sitting there in the dark, just waiting for him to wake up. How long had she been there? How long had he been here?

Ike began to take in his surroundings as the woman sat back in her chair. They were in what looked like a cellar although there were no foodstuffs to be seen. Only the clean earthy smell of potatoes hinted at the small room's previous occupation. The smell reminded Ike of how hungry he was. Ike had been hungry for days before he found himself in this place, whatever this place was, and he didn't know how long he had been here.

They had been looking for food, a commodity that was becoming scarce in northern Mississippi as two armies chased each other back and forth across the landscape. His regiment's supply lines had been cut by Chalmers' cavalry and they had been forced to live off a land that had already been "lived off" by their enemies.

The last semblance of a meal Ike recalled was when they had combined all the food they had, which had been some flour and cornmeal, and made crude rolls. Someone had come up with the idea of mixing the ground grain with water on a poncho and forming a sticky dough. They improvised ways of cooking it over the fire, some used green sticks, but the prevailing method became to impale it on their steel ramrods or bayonets and hold it above the coals until it was brown. Compared to hardtack it wasn't too awful as long as it was still warm. Johnny had them laughing as usual when he teased Sarge. "Hey Sarge, your roll looks like a horse turd. How do you like it?"

"Johnny, if I was any hungrier I'd probably eat a horse turd." Sarge replied, keeping the laughter going. Before long everyone was chuckling and joking about "horse turds" and making their rolls into more bizarre and obscene shapes, producing even more gales of laughter. Schoolboys playing hooky couldn't have had a much better time than Company D when they laughed together. Remembering better days with his friends brought back his fear for them. How many had died in the ambush?

"I suppose you must be hungry now." The woman said, staring at Ike in a way that he couldn't decipher.

"Yes Ma'am.....I don't know how long it's been." He said, trying to sound apologetic. For a brief moment something inside of him made him want to say "I'm hungry enough to eat a horse turd." He was appalled that such a thought would come to his mind. It was just the kind of thing Johnny O'Donnell would have said.

Ike had caught his Sergeant's distaste for foraging and wished he had the words to convey how reluctant he had been to pilfer food from civilians. "Military necessity," the Colonel had called it when he first assigned them the duty.

The old Colonel had been mortified when he had returned to his regiment from sick leave to find Company "G" clumsily butchering a stolen cow at the side of the road. He had wanted the men punished for their thievery but the Brigadier had looked at the cow and the men standing around it with their heads bowed in shame from the Colonel's outburst. The Colonel's superior cleared his throat to bring silence to the crowd and said "If I ever hear of any of my men doing such a piss-poor job of butchering again, I'll have the whole lot of you flogged. The officer climbed down off his horse, grabbed a knife from one of the soldiers and began dissecting the hind quarter of the animal with obvious skill. "Now this is how you carve a flank steak!"

The Colonel had not been able to look his men in the eye for a couple of days without betraying his sadness and dismay. A couple of more weeks of living on short rations or none at all and the Colonel overcame some of his qualms about "Jayhawking."

Of course there were those who saw "Military Necessity" as a license to take anything that wasn't nailed down and a good number of items that were. The only time Ike had ever seen Sarge really mad at one of his men was when he found out that Dan Clark had stolen a valise full of women's clothing. Sarge was a big man and normally easy going, but when he found Clark stowing the bag in the supply wagon and determined what was in it he lost his temper. Sarge punched and pummeled the soldier until he had to be pulled off of him by a couple of the other men. As soon as the Sergeant had calmed down a bit he had Clark marched back to the house where he had purloined the clothes.

The detail assigned to accompany Clark had great fun at the expense of their comrade who was carrying the valise and wearing a bonnet that had been found inside. As if this weren't enough Sarge had insisted that the soldier also carry the dainty parasol that had been found tucked away amidst the other clothes. Johnny O'Donnell had rolled on the ground and laughed his distinctive donkey bray as the small squad left the camp. Clark was in the lead and Sarge walked behind him delivering a kick or a prod if he lowered the parasol.

As much as most of the soldiers detested the "military necessity" of separating the locals from their foodstuffs, an army had to eat, and it was beginning to be seen that the sufferings of the general population might lead to their losing the will to continue the conflict. General Sherman's quote about war being hell was being brought home to the citizens of northern Mississippi. The Home Guard was fighting back and retaliating for what they saw as wanton theft.

As abhorrent as the "military necessity" of raiding the larders of civilians was, the wholesale slaughter of his fellow human beings was a "military necessity" that had left Ike far more sickened and scarred. He knew that men who he had known and loved had died in this woman's door yard, the question that hung over them was how many and which ones.

After staring at Ike for a few moments the woman called over her shoulder to an unseen presence. "Marcus, get him something to eat, I think mush will do for now."

"Yas'm." came a deep voice from behind the woman. Footsteps followed and a door creaked open letting moonlight in to illuminate the wooden steps going up to the cellar door. The massive shape of a man blocked out most of the light and then the door was closed, shutting out all but the light from the lamp.

The silence was disquieting to Ike as the woman resumed her stare.

"Ma'am?" Ike started.

"Yes." She replied.

"How long have I been here?"

"Two days. It was the day before yesterday that you and your companions attempted to pillage my farm."

"Two days..." Ike rasped, trying to think of what day it had been and what time of day he had last been conscious. "What time is it?" he asked.

"It should be around 4 O'clock in the morning, I thought I heard you stirring around 3 O'clock and came down here to see about you and I'm sure it has been at least an hour." As if in confirmation Ike heard a clock somewhere above striking four times.

"The home guard knew you were coming this way and lay in wait. For my part, I was against bloodshed in my own dooryard, but I had little choice, and I did not fancy having all my foodstuffs pilfered and I had no idea what other depredations might follow."

Ike was sure of and embarrassed for the "depredations" that the woman was referring to. There had been accusations of rape and looting by Union soldiers not long ago. There had been several men in the division flogged for looting and one was hanged for assaulting a woman. It was suddenly important to Ike for the woman to know that his own squad had only been interested in finding something to eat.

"I...I'm sorry, Ma'am." Ike wheezed. "We were starving." He realized how dry his mouth was. As if the woman had read his thoughts she handed him a cup.

"Drink this. It's water and a little brandy. Don't drink it too fast or it will come back up and I might not be inclined to give you more."

He took the cup and obediently sipped with care. The water cooled his parched mouth and the liquor warmed him deeper inside.

"Thank you, Ma'am." Ike replied between cautious sips. "I'm normally a Teetotaler, but that seems to have a medicinal effect." Ike lied. The warmth of the brandy was not an alien presence in any sense, but he instinctively implied otherwise.

"A little wine for thy stomach's sake and thine often infirmities." The woman said with no hesitation.

"1st Timothy 5:23." Ike responded, not too quickly he hoped. He knew his Bible well, but not as well as his response might have implied. He had used this verse often to justify his bouts of drinking to Emma and to himself. His "infirmities" were usually not too often, but had put a strain on his marriage.

The woman's expression remained as before, not betraying her reaction to his statement as he finished off the liquid in the cup.

The door creaked open again and broke the silence that followed Ike's scriptural exposition. Marcus placed a tray next to Ike's pallet on the floor and helped him sit up, turning him so that he could sit with his back propped against the stone wall and hold the warm bowl on his lap.

Ike had never been fond of mush. His family had endured some hard times in his very early youth and there was sometimes little else to eat and the memory of his childhood poverty usually clung to the humble fare. This mush, however assumed a flavor and texture that was marvelous. The splendor of it was partly because it had been so long since Ike had eaten anything and partly that this normally bland fare was accompanied by substances that had been missing from Ike's diet for weeks. There was butter in an exuberant quantity, and salt which had been missing from his diet for days and a sweetness that he thought was probably honey.

He forced himself to eat slowly and found it hard not to moan in ecstasy. Ike ate every last bite and resisted the urge to scrape out the last lingering smear on the inside of the bowl with his grimy fingers and lick the crockery and fingers clean.

"Thank you." He said, quietly looking first at the woman and then at Marcus. The man was an enormous brown mountain.

Ike's experience with the ebony race was recent. The first Negroes he had ever seen had been the field slaves who had cheered and sang to them as they had marched west from Corinth after Beauregard's stealthy retreat. These people were something new and exotic to most of the men in the ranks. Free blacks had been banned from Illinois several years ago and slavery had long been forbidden.

The soldiers had laughed at the antics of the children as they brought buckets of cool water. Johnny openly ogled a young slave woman whose worn dress was so thin as to reveal enticing details of her shapely figure to a young man whose lust had become legendary. "Eyes forward, jackass!" Sarge had barked as Johnny marched forward with his head twisted nearly backward for one last leer. As more and more slaves walked away from their lives of servitude and attached themselves to the Union Army, Johnny managed a few attachments of his own.

The man looking down at Ike seemed to be old, but Ike could not place just how old he might have been. Marcus looked solid and strong, only the wrinkles in his otherwise flawless skin and the trace of white in the wool over his ears betrayed long years. The way that Marcus looked at him was not unkind but it made Ike uncomfortable. His gaze was almost as inscrutable as that of the woman but something in the way the towering vassal looked at Ike seemed to convey pity.

Marcus knelt and took the bowl and spoon gently from Ike's hands, he then handed the soldier a damp cloth and a bowl of water. Ike bathed his face and hands and relished the feel of being even a little clean after weeks of living in filth. He returned the now grimy cloth to Marcus and tried to convey his gratitude with a smile that was not returned.

"That is all for now, Marcus." The woman said.

"Yas'm." Marcus rumbled and turned to leave. Ike noted that the big man could just barely stand erect in the cellar. The nappy hair brushed the beams in places as he took his leave.

"Do you feel better?" the woman asked after Marcus had closed the door.

In spite of the pain in his leg and head, Ike was feeling almost giddy, his first inclination had been to respond "Yas'm." but he thought better of it.

"Yes Ma'am, I thank you kindly. I don't know what I can do to repay your kindness, but I intend to try as soon as I can." Ike said as earnestly as he could. His gratitude was sincere, the food and drink had done much to restore him.

"We will talk more tomorrow. For now you should sleep." She said, standing and picking up the lamp. She walked toward the door and as she reached the first step it opened outward for her. Marcus held it open as his mistress daintily ascended the steps. When the woman had cleared the door it shut again leaving Ike once more in total darkness.

He lay back down and adjusted himself on his blanket. The food and the small amount of brandy, which Ike believed might have been the best he had ever tasted, had left him feeling satisfied and for now he felt safe. He slept soundly and had no more dreams that he could recall.

A thin line of light was visible along the edge of the door on the hinged side when he awoke. A single ray came through a knot hole near the center of the door and painted a spot on the floor pale yellow, helping to illuminate Ike's new abode. As his eyes adjusted he carefully turned his head from side to side to allow him to take stock of his surroundings. The stonework of the cellar was finely done, the joints were mortared with extreme care and the walls were nearly perfect. The flagstone floor was level and relatively smooth. Above him were heavy timber beams that he assumed supported a house. He pictured the house as he had seen it before the ambush. Something about the appearance of the building had spoken to him even as he was reeling from the heat in the yard. The house looked like something of substance and permanence. It actually had a recent coat of paint unlike most of the houses they had seen in the south. He thought of Emma and of how she would love a house like this. He tried to remember their own home and could only remember small details of it and that it had somehow been a disappointment to them. He thought of how he would love to be able to give his wife a home like this. The reality of sleeping in such a permanent structure, even in its cellar, struck him as something amazing. After months of sleeping in the open in all kinds of weather surrounded by snoring, belching, and farting soldiers the quiet coolness of this cellar was agreeable.

He sat up carefully to see if his head would swim as it had previously. It did, but it was not as badly as before. He sat with his back against the wall and his legs stretched out before him and noted how neatly the splint had been applied to his left leg. Army doctors would have not done nearly as well in immobilizing the leg, but Army doctors were usually operating with the sound of cannons, small arms, and the screaming of dying men assailing their ears.

The chair and small table remained and Ike had an urge to sit in the chair. He couldn't remember the last time he has sat on an actual chair. Hard tack crates, chunks of firewood, and rocks had served as furniture for the last two years when he could even find such amenities. Often the best one could do was to sit cross legged on the ground. Real furniture seemed like something remarkable. Standing up made him light headed for a moment but he braced his hands against the wall until the feeling passed and hobbled over to occupy the seat where the woman had watched him......she had sat there in the dark for a full hour. Why had she bothered? The chair felt good, it made Ike feel more human to be sitting on something actually made for that purpose.

He jumped at what seemed like the sound of the echoing laughter that he had heard before, he looked around and listened to see if he could discern where it had come from, he could hear nothing from the outside and the sound seemed to have been too faint to have come from his new abode. The only thing he heard for certain was the clock striking eight from somewhere above. As he strained to hear where the laughter might have come from another matter arose to distract him.

It came to Ike that he couldn't remember having emptied his bladder in nearly three days and the urge was becoming pressing. He wondered if he had wet his uniform, but it was so sweat soaked and filthy that it would have been hard to determine. Dehydration had made passing water less of an issue until now. He was wondering if there was a corner in the cellar that would be any more acceptable than another when the door creaked open and Marcus entered carrying an enameled chamber pot and a crutch.

"Missy say you prob'ly be needin' this 'bout now." Marcus said, lifting the chamber pot.

"She must be a wise woman, Marcus, I am about to explode." Ike said, hoping to get a smile out of the taciturn giant who was helping him to his feet. Getting no reaction, Ike finished his business, marveling at how good it felt to empty his bladder. In civilian life he would have had a hard time voiding himself with someone else watching, but two years of passing water with so many others in attendance had rid him of that problem. He was usually glad to finish without someone else wetting down his shoes.

"Made that crutch fo' one of Missy's boys when he fell off'n a hoss and broke his leg a few years back." Marcus said. Something about his manner made Ike think that he was saddened by the recollection. The crutch was made of oak, with a thick heavy head that fit nicely under Ike's arm. The head had been carefully smoothed for the comfort of its user. The shaft was made from a tree limb nearly as thick as Ike's wrist and the length was perfect for Ike's build. The bark had been removed and it also had been shaved with obvious care.

Marcus went back out, closing the door behind him and returned a few minutes later with the chamber pot, which had been emptied out and rinsed, hanging from his elbow by its bale. He also carried the tray with a water pitcher and bowl along with the drinking cup, another bowl of what he assumed was more mush also occupied the tray. The tray was placed on the table and the chamber pot was relegated to the corner of the cellar farthest from the door. Marcus gave a small bow and went back up the steps, closing the door behind him. Ike noticed the sound of something heavy being placed on the door after the big man's exit.

Ike attacked the bowl, which he discovered contained oatmeal with cream and a few fresh blackberries on top. This time he did lick the whole concern clean and let out a belch that felt wonderful. He washed it all down with water from the ewer and proceeded to wash himself as thoroughly as he could with the remaining water and a sliver of soap which smelled to him of lavender.

The soap smell reminded him of Emma. He closed his eyes and pictured her sitting on their bed after a bath brushing out her hair. His loins began to quiver as his mind's eye wandered over the delights of the young woman on his bed. Ike opened his eyes and shook his head to sweep the image of Emma from his consciousness; much more of this would just be torture.

He tried to focus his mind on his situation. His squad had been ambushed while foraging at the woman's house. He had accidentally avoided being killed by having gone for water to cool his fever and had been grazed by a bullet that was meant to kill him and fell and cracked his leg while seeking cover during the assault. The homeowner had taken him in and was caring for him and nursing him back to health. Why was she doing this?

Something told him that the blow to his head had affected his mind. He remembered that he was married to Emma, but he could not remember her maiden name or their wedding. He remembered that he had a brother who had died at Shiloh, but could not remember his face or much of their childhood. The scars on his hands and arms looked like they might have been burns but he had no recollection of how they came to be. Most disturbing of all was the feeling that he wasn't alone here and the snatches of laughter that seemed to echo in his mind. He sat still and listened for the voice that seemed to call his name from time to time but there was nothing. He finally managed to focus on the reality of where he was at present.

Ike was formulating questions he wanted to ask when the door creaked open and he heard the woman's voice. "Are you decent?"

"Yes Ma'am." Ike responded, instinctively standing up with the aid of the crutch as the woman appeared. His head swam again, but he managed to recover and remain upright.

She came down the stairs followed by Marcus, who was carrying another chair. The second chair was placed facing the one already present. Marcus went back up the steps without speaking but did not close the door. The sunlight relieved the gloom and warmed Ike's body and to a lesser extent his spirit.

"Please sit down." The woman said indicating the second chair. "Your break was not bad, but you need to keep that leg elevated for a while. You lost quite a bit of blood from your head wound and you will be weak for a few days"

At that Marcus appeared again carrying a small footstool in one hand and another tray in the other. The footstool was placed in front of Ike and the tray replaced the previous one on the small table. Marcus went back up the steps with the first tray after gently placing Ike's left foot on the stool.

"Would you like some coffee?" she said, pouring from a china vessel into one of the cups. "There isn't much real coffee in it. I have extended my supply by adding chicory, but it is the best I have for now."

"Thank you, we've been out of coffee for days since the...... since our supply lines were interrupted."

He took the cup from her and waited as she poured her own. He waited for her to take the first sip out of a sense of decorum. He also had a nagging fear that she might try to drug him.

The ersatz coffee was not bad. The chicory added an earthy flavor that was not unpleasant. Compared to the outlandishly strong brew that he was used to being served up by his Sergeant this coffee was excellent. She watched him as he sipped the dark liquid.

"I suppose you have questions about what happened."

"Yes Ma'am I do. Particularly about my squad, did anyone survive except me?"

"Your Sergeant and the big blond fellow who was at his elbow escaped unharmed. They were close to my house and weren't fired on. Four of your men are buried next to my garden and several were apparently wounded but were able to get away. You were overlooked and indeed Marcus and I didn't notice you until sometime later."

Ike was relieved to hear that Sarge and Billy were alive, he thought of asking her to describe the dead men, but grief, fear, and uncertainty made him hold his tongue for the moment.

As if she had read his thoughts the woman said "I will describe the ones we buried, one was short with red hair, two had coal black hair and beards and looked like brothers, and there was a fellow with light brown hair and freckles who wore glasses. Marcus and I said a prayer over their graves and gave them what dignity we could. I am sorry, I suppose they were your friends."

"Yes, the little red haired fellow was my tent mate; he was a character......." Ike said, holding back a sob. "I didn't know the others as well, but we went through a lot together." He had to close his eyes as he thought of Johnny lying buried close by. Johnny would no longer be teasing Sarge and his other comrades and singing and dancing with the contrabands. Johnny who had loved and enjoyed life to an extent Ike sometimes envied but couldn't always approve of would never again go "a wenchin'" as he called his nocturnal forays. Ike imagined the young Negro women keening over the young man who had paid them so much attention.

It seemed that he could remember more about Johnny than he could about himself. Like a lot of the people who inhabited the southern end of his home state of Illinois, the O'Donnell's had come from the south. Only one generation from Ireland they were small time farmers and sharecroppers. They had not been able to compete with the slave holding planters and had moved farther north to free soil. While they were not prosperous, they eked out a living and held a grudge against the system of slave labor that they blamed for having kept them down.

Ike had first met Johnny at Camp Butler, where their regiment had been sent to train as the war was erupting. He had resented having to share a tent with this loud illiterate, whose very purpose in life seemed to be amusing himself at someone else's expense. Little by little, the two had become close friends. Johnny was outspoken and gregarious while Ike was quiet and reserved. Ike came to realize that other than his brother and later on his wife, he had never been as close to anyone as he had become with Johnny. Long and sometimes one sided conversations revealed a young man with many of the same insecurities and fears that Ike had. Ike was devastated that two of the people that meant the most to him were now gone and Emma was so far out of his reach as to be nearly lost to him as well.

Johnny had said that he enlisted so he could go back and whip the "nigger drivers" that had kept his family poor. He also admitted that he didn't care much for farming and thirteen dollars a month plus food and clothing looked like a better prospect than staying home. As the two of them became closer Johnny confided that if he had stayed around home much longer a certain young woman was likely to become pregnant. "I just knowed we'd end up married and have a whole herd of young 'uns and she'd end up lookin' like her 'ma and outweighin' me. Sleepin' in a tent with you fellers ain't so bad when I think about th' alternative." He had said. Ike wished he could remember his own motives for joining the army.

Ike decided to mourn his comrades at a later time when he was alone with his thoughts. He was beginning to suspect that he would have ample time soon enough. He looked down at his leg as he thought about his squad members and decided he should change the subject. "I appreciate how well you attended to my leg."

"My late husband was a doctor. I assisted him at a great many things. Your leg seems to have only a very small fracture so I didn't have to set it. You should be able to walk on it in a few weeks if you behave yourself."

"Then I suppose I will just have to behave myself." Ike replied with a smile, hoping to get another in return. The woman's expression still didn't change.

"My head wound.....is it deep?"

"No, it seems the bullet just grazed your skull, there was a lot of bruising and a small fracture and indentation but it did not penetrate the skull itself. I fear there will be a permanent scar. Why do you ask?"

"My memories seem....disorganized, I remember some things but not others. It is disturbing to me that I can't seem to remember what I did for a living before the war, or what my wife's maiden name was."

"Do you remember your name young man?"

"Isaac Lowery Ma'am, from Florence, Illinois, most people call me Ike. At least I remember Florence, as small as it is." He smiled at the fact that he could recollect his home, but again the smile was not returned. "Might I have the pleasure of you name?"

"I am Mrs. Micheline Pendleton. You may address me as Mrs. Pendleton."

"Thank you, Mrs. Pendleton, for everything. I appreciate that you haven't turned me in to the Confederate authorities......" he said as the thought and its accompanying question (why?) entered his mind.

"I gave it a good deal of thought young man, but I expect you would have not been well cared for and there has been enough suffering here for now. I prayed about what to do with you and I believe I have an answer. I assume you are a praying man Mr. Lowery?"

"Yes Ma'am, I am. I think I have prayed more fervently in the last few months than at any period in my life." Ike responded, he had clear memories of conversations with God during gunfire. Though he remembered that he and Emma were churchgoers, it seemed that his beliefs had been more academic and theoretical before his life had been in so much peril.

"In my case, I believe I have been favored with a sign, Mr. Lowery." The woman said with her back to him. "I have been asking for God to show me that I have not been forgotten. Have you ever been angry with God, Mr. Lowery?"

Ike thought for a moment as he carefully sifted through his remaining memories and replied "Only once Mrs. Pendleton, when I lost someone dear to me. I can't say as I am still angry, I can't even remember who it was, but...." He paused, unsure of himself and trying to analyze why he could so vividly remember being angry, but not whose loss had triggered his anger. "I just remember being angry....but I believe his ways are above our ways and maybe I will understand some day."

This time she looked at him with more interest. Ike thought there might have been emotion in her face as she turned to address him again.

"I too have lost people dear to me, nearly everyone. Four of my sons have died in this war. Gunshot and disease have taken four of my dear sons. My poor husband had a stroke and eventually died of grief when we were told of the last one. I have one son left, Mr. Lowery, do you have any children?"

"Not yet Ma'am." He replied thinking of how Emma longed to have children and how they had begun to be afraid that there would be none as she failed to conceive.

"They are a gift from God...... a gift he sometimes takes away. In my case I think he took my sons as a punishment."

"A punishment?"

"You see, my husband actively promoted this war. He helped raise a regiment and donated money for arms and uniforms. He encouraged our sons to enlist. His belief in the glorious cause brought us nothing but grief.

Being a dutiful wife, I went along with his wishes, although I had reservations."

"So you believe that God is against the Southern cause?"

"I did for a while, but as I read and comprehended the news I came to the understanding that young men on both sides are dying in virtually equal numbers. God is punishing us all for our pride and foolishness.....in *equal numbers*!" She accentuated the last two words in a tone that startled Ike.

"You said you were shown a sign." Ike said.

"Yes dear boy, yes! It came to me so clearly and gave me great hope." She said, looking at the sky beyond the open cellar door. "The numbers......the numbers...."

"You saw numbers?" Ike asked, half thinking that if he could see the patch of sky the woman was gazing at he would see strings of numbers writ in cloud.

"Four dead boys in my side yard....four Union soldiers.....to atone for my poor lambs slain in the struggle." She turned her gaze from the sky back to Ike. "My four beautiful sons are buried in lonely graves far from home and I have been sent four others to bury in their stead." She said, taking a breath and looked back up at the sky as if she were addressing it. "And one living, left for me to minister to, to care for so that God will keep my last son alive." She quickly turned to Ike and moved her face close to his, searching his expression for understanding. "Mr. Lowery, you have been sent here by God! Can you not feel it?" Her face glowed with animation that Ike wouldn't have thought possible moments before. "Todd's last letter came day before yesterday from a field hospital where he is recovering from a head wound and a minor fracture almost identical to your own! I intend to keep you here and care for you until this foolishness is over and Todd returns safely to his home. Marcus and I will care for your every need, we have food stored safely away in a well hidden location and Marcus is a skilled gardener and hunter. You will be kept comfortable and well fed as my assurance to God of my intentions. I believe that in return my Son will be safe in spite of this horrid war."

Mrs. Pendleton gazed into Ike's eyes and her expression of joy intensified even further.

"Mr. Lowery, your eyes are the same shade of blue as Todd's! If I wasn't convinced before that you were sent here purposefully, I am now!"

"Well, I........" Ike said, finding himself at a loss for anything else to say. The cellar had started to warm from the sunlight shining down through the open door but Ike felt chilled, he swayed in his chair and closed his eyes to think about all he had just heard.

Ike heard the laughter again, this time he recognized Johnny O'Donnell's cackle in his head "Hey Ikey, you look like somebody just walked across your grave! That big nigger just walked over mine!" Ike flinched and looked around to see if anyone else had heard Johnny.

"Mr. Lowery are you alright?" the woman said with a sudden concern in her voice.

"Just a little chill, I think......" Ike said, despairing that he was losing his sanity. He was also convinced that Mrs. Pendleton's mind had been damaged by her losses. He wasn't sure which bothered him the worst or put him in the most peril. He closed his eyes and tried to make sense of it all. It came to him that he might still be dreaming. He looked up and saw that Marcus had come back down the stairs.

"Ikey, you're the luckiest guy they is! Them purty blue eyes of yours are just the ticket! You get to sit out the rest of the war in that there cellar. I'm stuck out there in the side yard feedin' the flowers." Johnny's voice continued in a nasal snicker.

"Mr. Lowery, I think you should lie down for a while." The woman said, taking Ike by the arm. "Marcus, please help Mr. Lowery to his pallet."

The light from outside was eclipsed as Marcus descended the steps. Ike noted how quietly he moved for someone his size. Graceful, graceful like a cat, something in the big man's actions reminded Ike of the huge black Tom that his mother had once fed. The cat was gentle with Ike and his brother, but would kill any other cat that dared come close to the house.

His head still swimming, Ike was gently placed back on his pallet on the floor. The finest feather pillow he had ever come in contact with was slipped under his head and he was covered with a handmade quilt. Ike puzzled about where they came from and decided that Marcus had been in the process of bringing them already.

The woman's hand rested on his forehead for a couple of seconds. She looked relieved not to find him feverish. She turned and said something to Marcus that Ike couldn't hear and then returned her attention to him. "You are still suffering from being overheated and from blood loss due to your head wound Mr. Lowery, rest now and we will talk more later. I believe we have much to discuss. Rest assured that you will be well cared for and returned to your loved ones as soon as this war is over and my son returns safely to me." Her smile was radiant, but it did not comfort the man on the floor. Behind that smile lurked something that Ike could not put a name to. He closed his eyes partly from exhaustion and partly to avoid looking at Micheline Pendleton's disturbing countenance. Consciousness began to drift away as the woman and her companion exited up the steps. Johnny O'Donnell's voice brought him back awake when the door was closed.

"Fine pillow there Ikey, beats the dickens out of the ole' tree root my skulls a layin' on. I think you're a gonna have you a nice easy spell......unless somethin' happens to her boy." Johnny trailed of giggling.

"Shut up Johnny!" Ike's mind retorted. He looked up to make sure he hadn't spoken out loud in the hearing of his hostess. Hostess...... was that the proper word? Was Mrs. Pendleton his hostess or his jailer?

"Is she your hostess, your jailer, or your new Mama?" Johnny chortled. "She might just take care of you in all sorts of ways old pard. She's still mighty fine lookin' woman wouldn't you say?"

"Johnny, please don't torment me like that. I was about to pray for your soul, but I'm beginning to think it's no use."

"Oh Ikey, you was always the serious one. Don't worry so much, I'm just one of them waaaaaanderin' sheep the preachers always talk about. The shepherd'll be by to get me sometime but for now I'm supposed to watch over you."

"Wonderful! Emma always talked about guardian angels watching over us. It stands to reason that I would get a guardian angel like you."

Johnny laughed raucously and replied. "Nobody ever give me a harp or any wings yet. Don't know if I'll ever be an angel but so far bein' dead's kinda' entertainin'…. like a stage show where I can watch you and your lady friend and old 'Uncle Tom' a follerin' her around a steppin' and fetchin'."

"I hope the shepherd comes to get you pretty soon, I need some sleep."

"Well, I can be still for a while, maybe I oughta' sing you a lullaby." Johnny's voice crooned and then burst into a gale of braying laughter.

"Teacher!" Johnny blurted out as if he had just thought of something important. "You was a schoolteacher. Maybe that's part of what I'm here for is to help you remember stuff. I never did think you was a tellin' me everthin' but you said you was a teacher. You was a 'headmaster' at a little school there in

Florence. You taught the little 'uns readin, writin', and 'rithmetic. You even taught me some, an' I never was much of a student."

"Are you sure Johnny? I don't remember." Ike was disturbed by this revelation. He couldn't remember being a teacher, but somehow it seemed like Johnny knew. The snatches of poetry in his dream, recited by children seemed to connect to what Johnny was saying, but Ike could not remember actually teaching. It was disturbing how real his invisible companion seemed. Ike despaired that his head wound might have done serious damage.

Mercifully Ike drifted off again, worn out by his conversations with the living and the dead.

Sometime in what Ike imagined was early afternoon the door creaked open and woke the slumbering soldier from a restful near dreamless sleep. Again Marcus was carrying the tray with the pitcher and cup and a bowl with eating utensils. The bowl contained a rich stew with chunks of chicken and vegetables. Ike sat and ate with relish as the big man watched with apparent satisfaction. When Ike was halfway through the stew Marcus turned and started up the stairs. "Be back." He said over his shoulder as Ike discovered that the folded cloth at the side of the bowl contained a biscuit that had been split and buttered.

"You're a gonna' get fatter'n the old chaplain there Ikey! That ol' gal's a gonna plump you up right good for somethin'." Johnny chortled.

Ike was eating and ignoring Johnny when Marcus returned with a bucket of warm water, more soap, towels, and a nightshirt.

"Missy want me to get you cleaned up."

"Do you think I might need it?" earned Ike a small smile from the brown giant.

Ike cooperated and helped as best he could as Marcus removed his uniform, which was rank from days of marching in the Mississippi heat. The big man gently scrubbed him from head to toe without an unnecessary word. The splint was removed temporarily and replaced after Ike had been clothed in the nightshirt that Marcus said "useta' b'long ta' one of Missy's boys."

"You just sit here and rest a bit. Be right back." Marcus said, bundling up Ike's clothing, the tray and its contents and the bucket effortlessly as he headed back up the steps.

"My my but you smell good Ikey! Cain't say as I'm a smellin' too good myself right now. Gettin' kinda' rotten out there in my hole."

"You always were kind of rotten Johnny." Ike responded in his head. The ongoing conversation with his dead comrade was becoming natural to him. Whether Johnny was a figment of his imagination caused by the trauma to his head or a genuine guardian angel the familiar voice was becoming a strange comfort. He was chatting internally with Johnny when Marcus returned with the tray which now carried shaving implements and a mirror.

"Don't slip and cut your throat with that there razor, Ikey! Mama Pendleton needs you alive so she can trade you to God for her boy."

Ike did manage to nick himself at the thought Johnny had put in his head. Marcus automatically put a cloth soaked in witch hazel to his neck until the small wound was stanched.

"Careful 'dere sodjur, Massa's ole' blade still purty sharp." Marcus said as he examined Ike's neck. Satisfied that his charge was not bleeding to death, he actually smiled at Ike as he took the tray and implements back up the steps. "Missy be down shawtly."

Marcus' shadow had barely cleared the top step when Micheline Pendleton's form glided down them with still another tray. A pot of tea and more biscuits along with some excellent jam resided on this smaller tray which appeared to be made of silver.

"My boys loved my muscadine jam. It appears that it agrees with you as well." The woman said with a smile.

"This is very good." Ike said swallowing carefully so as not to speak with his mouth full. His hostess seemed to be genuinely pleased to see him eat well. Ike saw what an attractive woman she had been and still was when happiness softened the stern set of her features.

"I was just remembering how Todd looked with jam all over his face once when he sneaked down here and gobbled up an entire jar before Marcus caught him." She looked quietly around as if she could see a young boy getting up to mischief. "The poor child was sick for two days from having gorged himself." She said barely holding back a girlish giggle.

"I received a letter from Todd today." The woman said, her tone more sober. "He has recovered from his wounds and is riding with General Forrest and seems to be having a splendid time. A few days ago that news would have been devastating, but now I know he can have his fun and come home safely to take his rightful place here." Her smile remained pleasing, but her eyes seemed to be dilated to the point that the pupils were pools of black. Ike thought she was trembling slightly. He began to feel a tremor of his own.

"Toddy will surely be safe with Nathan Bedford Forrest!" Johnny gushed. "Why I hear he puts all his boys to bed just after dark and reads them a story ever night! Yep, ol' Forrest takes gooooood care of his boys.......when he ain't havin' em ride into artillery! Remember how cautiously he charged into us back at Fallen Timbers?   But now that you're here that boy's bullet proof! Why he can catch cannonballs and jus' throw 'em back!"

The biscuit and jam seemed to coalesce into a small hard lump that sat stubbornly in Ike's midsection, refusing to digest. The formerly pleasant aftertaste soured in his mouth. He took a long sip of the hot tea to wash down the taste and settle his stomach. He was afraid he might be as sick on the jam as Todd had been. The action of drinking the tea also bought him a few moments to reflect on how he should respond to Mrs. Pendleton's last statement. He was at a loss for words and Johnny's contribution was of no help.

Ike thought of how Forrest's cavalry "had their fun" back in Tennessee. The General had recklessly charged his men into the teeth of an infantry brigade and nearly lost his own life in the process. Bedford Forrest's idea of fun got people killed. In spite of being shot in the back at close range Forrest had managed to grab a hapless infantryman and swing him across the back of his saddle for a human shield of sorts. The big man rode off with his screaming hostage bouncing behind him like a rag doll. When they were out of range the young soldier was flung off the horse like unnecessary baggage. The victim's neck was broken when he slammed against one of the scattered tree trunks that the engagement would be remembered by. Forrest himself had incredibly recovered, but people around him were not usually as fortunate. Forrest left a trail of blue and gray clad corpses wherever he rode, and the man rode often.

Marcus broke what had become an uncomfortable silence when he came down the steps carrying a bed frame. Carrying the heavy oak frame looked like it would have been a chore for two men, but Mrs. Pendleton's vassal made the job look effortless. Ike hadn't noticed that the straw and blanket had been removed while he was enjoying his afternoon tea. The frame was placed where the pallet had been with the head in the corner. Marcus headed back up the steps.

"I thought you might be more comfortable and recuperate faster if you had a decent bed." Mrs. Pendleton said. "This was Todd's and it will be again someday. I hope you enjoy it."

The thought of sleeping on an actual bed was almost unbelievable to Ike as he watched the civilized furnishings being assembled for his use. It had been two years since his slumbers had been supported by anything softer than an army blanket and some leaves. He and his comrades had slept in railroad cars and on the decks of river steamers but never on so much as a rude cot since he had left home. One night he and Johnny had slept on a brush pile to avoid the mud and the water of a creek that was backing up into their camp.

Marcus returned with a feather mattress and placed it on the frame. He had sheets and a comforter over one massive arm and prepared the bed as Ike watched with a mix of emotions.

"Looks like you oughta' sleep like a baby there Ikey!" Johnny chimed in. "Wonder why she just didn't move you upstairs? Sure woulda been less work for ol' Marcus. Wonder why that big buck never run off, reckon he's takin' care of Missy in other ways?"

"You look tired again Mr. Lowery, would you like to lie down and rest a while before supper?"

"Thank you Mrs. Pendleton, I think I would. Your kindness is......"

"You are quite welcome young man. It is our Christian duty to care for those who are ailing and infirm, but I do have more selfish reasons as you know. I will return later."

The bed seemed to swallow Ike as he lay down. He closed his eyes and prayed, for guidance, for healing, and for Todd Pendleton wherever he was.

"Yeah, Ikey, I think you better pray for that young fella' cause if somethin' happens to that boy his momma' might not be bringin' you no more biscuits and jam."

"Johnny, I'm trying to pray here, you shouldn't be interrupting me." Ike grumbled at the voice. He was beginning to tire of the constant commentary and wondered again if it was a sign of some mental problem on his part.

"Sorry Ike, I'm new to this 'guardian angel' duty. I kinda think I took on somebody that needs some real guardin'."

Ike continued to pray. He asked God to help him maintain his sanity and for Johnny's voice to go away.

"Aw come on now, I'm just doin' my job the best I know how." Johnny said in a mock simper. "Just lay down yer' head to sleep now and your guardian angel's gonna stand picket. You're safe......fer now. 'Til that ol' gal gets another letter anyway."

Supper was roast chicken and potatoes with a slice of dried apple pie. His hostess was chatty and took her supper in the cellar with her guest. Afterwards she read to Ike from the Bible. She was on the book of Job on her latest sojourn through the scriptures.

"I sometimes feel a kinship with Job, having lost so many in my family. But I think it is my least favorite book in the Bible. Do you have a favorite part, Mr. Lowery?"

"Well, it definitely wouldn't be Job. I always felt like God and Satan were playing a game with him. I don't like to think of God like that, he just seems cruel and disinterested in Job's suffering. I guess I like the epistles of Paul as well as anything. I like his way with words." Ike had always been impressed by the apostle's colorful prose with his imagery of gongs booming and cymbals clashing and how he talked about seeing "through a glass darkly." He paused for a moment and his mind wandered back to happier times. "When Emma and I were first married, we read from the Song of Solomon together. Emma would get the giggles sometimes....."

"You miss your wife terribly." She said looking down.

"Yes, we have been apart for so long....." Ike replied trailing off. His memories of Emma were vivid in some ways but sketchy in others. It was as if his mind was a book and some of the pages had been torn out. He briefly wanted to share those thoughts with Mrs. Pendleton, but decided to keep his reserve. Her book seemed to be a nightmare tale and he was sure that he would have liked to have not been a part of this or any chapter. They both were quiet for a few moments.

"When you are united to the right person, parting is painful. I miss my husband Jasper every day. In a way I miss him more than our sons." She paused, sighed, and then brightened. "But let us not dwell on our losses, in your case at least you will see your Emma again I'm sure and I will have Todd by my side in my dotage. We must be thankful to the Lord for the blessings we have. All we have to do is keep you healthy and safe. Now you must do your part by getting a good night's sleep." She rose at this and looked down at him with a soft smile.

"I always liked that part about old Balaam." Johnny interjected as Mrs. Pendleton left the cellar. "You know, that feller that got the talkin' too from his ass? My brothers and I got tickled when the preacher said ass in church."

"I am beginning to think that God sent me a talking ass." Ike responded silently as Johnny went into hysterics and made braying noises.

Chapter 2 – The Babylonian Captivity

The days that followed took on a routine and went by dreamily as Ike's hurts healed. He was well fed by Marcus and given a clean nightshirt and water for a bath on a regular basis. Jasper Pendleton had accumulated an extensive library and Ike was allowed to read one volume at a time by the light from the knothole during the day and by candle light at night. Marcus delivered him a new book every few days as he worked his way through the Pendleton's favorite authors. He was also given an old Bible to keep in his room. Ike was never given matches, but Marcus lit the candle every evening at supper time and made sure he had a fresh one when needed. Mrs. Pendleton usually took his evening meal with him and read to him from the Bible afterwards. Their conversations were polite but never deep.

Sundays were church days. Mrs. Pendleton came down late morning and read scripture and a homily from a book. They sang common hymns like "Shall we Gather at the River", "Amazing Grace", "Happy Land of Canaan", and "What a Friend We Have in Jesus". Marcus' deep rumbling baritone and Mrs. Pendleton's tenor carried Ike's weak alto. Johnny sang along in Ike's head.

Ike tried to keep track of the time by marking how many Sundays he had been in the cellar. He made a small mark on the back of one of the steps after every service, but he wasn't sure how many weeks he had been here before the services began. It seemed that it must be October by his reckoning and by the cooler but still mild weather. He could begin to see some color in the few trees that were visible through his knot hole.

Johnny was a near constant presence, commenting on everything and seemingly finding much humor in Ike's situation.

"Still like being dead, Johnny?" Ike asked one day when boredom was setting in.

"Not too bad Ikey, company could be better though" he snickered.

"I've been thinking lately. Since you say you're not exactly an angel, are you a ghost?"

"Ooooh Ikey, I always been afeard of ghosties!" Johnny replied trying to sound ominous and then paused. "I don't know too much and if I did I don't think I could tell you a whole lot. I just know that I ain't afraid of anything anymore. I know my time of fear an pain is over and there's better yet to come. I don't just believe it or think it, I *know* it. I'm just a livin' in your head for now and waitin'. Somethin' about it kinda' reminds me of somethin' my old Irish Papist Grandma' used to talk about, now what did she call it? Started with a "P"......porky.....perky.....perkytory I think it was."

"Purgatory." Ike corrected him. "The Catholics believe that when you die with sin on your soul you are sent to a temporary place where your remaining unforgiven sins are washed away so that you will be pure before your final entry into heaven." Ike had always liked the idea although his Methodist faith officially saw it as a pagan heresy.

"Yeah, I think that was what she called it. My folks had parted ways with the Papists, but Granny still said her beads and read from her prayer book she brought with her from Ireland after the 'tater famine and ignored it when my folks tried to get her to go to their church and get sanctified. I think Granny was as sanctified as anybody I ever knowed, the old girl loved us kids, even me, an' love's what's important, I know that for a fact."

"So you're in my head being purified before you move on?"

"Somethin' like that. Your head's kinda cramped though, lots of cobwebs up here and some ol' mud dobber nests like somebody's attic." Johnny said with a giggle.

"Well get used to it. As I recall the soul in Purgatory had to stay longer if they were stained with too much sin. I may be stuck with you for a long time."

Johnny laughed a laugh that sounded like his old guffaw from back in camp but with a tone that sounded gentler. It wasn't the laugh of derision but a laugh of joy. "It may take a while Ikey, but what's time to a ghost or an angel, or whatever I am?"

"Were you a churchgoer back home Johnny?" Ike asked. "I didn't see you at the chaplain's services very often.

"Guess I'd become what you'd call a backslider, Ike. I sat in the anxious seat and got prayed over a couple times back home, but I was never sure it really took 'til I started goin' to the Nigger services back there in Memphis. I know the rest of you thought I was just a flirtin' and wenchin' with them brown beauties. I started out that way but then this one girl, she musta' been a African princess, she insisted I go to a meetin' with her. Ikey, that there girl was beautiful as any white girl I ever seen, her skin was so perfect an' smooth and her eyes were so big you could just get lost in 'em. She seemed to think I was funny and laughed at most of my jokes, but she wouldn't sneak out in the woods with me like some did. She wasn't mean about it or anythin' she would just pat me on the cheek and smile and shake her head. One day she told me to come out to the woods with her, only it was to this big prayer meetin'. Them folks treated me like I was one of their own, they had me singin' and a dancin' with them, even if I couldn't dance so good as they did. I never saw so much joy at a church service in all my life. Before I knowed it I was gettin' baptized by this big ol' buck of a preacher. Ikey, I felt closer to God among those Darkies than I ever did at a white service."

Ike imagined Johnny being lowered into a creek by a gargantuan preacher that resembled Marcus. "How long did the preacher hold you under?" he said out loud with a chuckle.

"Just long enough, Ikey, just long enough. I knowed I was different when he drew me back out of that water. I looked around me at all them folks, half expectin' that they was havin' a good laugh at my red headed self a drippin like a drowned rat and all I saw was people that loved me. I sorta' understand what Momma Pendleton thinks about God puttin' people in the right place at the right time, I know he put me in Memphis for a good reason, and I'm sure he put me here for a good reason too."

The two were quiet for a while and then Ike remembered what he had been meaning to ask Johnny. He chastised himself for taking these conversations so seriously, but he couldn't help himself. His eyes were tired from reading "Ivanhoe" by the light from the knothole.

"Johnny, what was dying like?"

"Oh Ikey, it was awful! I've had some pain in my life, but bein shot where I was hurt somethin fierce."

"Where were you hit?"

"In the front yard!" Johnny said laughing so hard it made Ike's head hurt. Johnny was having a good time telling his story.

"Well, let's just say if I'd lived I wouldn't be doin anymore wenchin'. Sorry to say that was my first thought before the pain really set in, I was mortified that my manhood was so mangled up. One of them Graybacks managed to put a round through my head while I was standin' there hollerin' and mournin' the loss of my favorite parts and the pain stopped. I came to and found myself just a floatin' over that mess of flesh that used to be ol' Johnny O'Donnell. As odd as it was, I wasn't scared or anythin'. I was just glad to be outa' the pain. Hard to explain it Ikey, but it wasn't just the pain of havin' my privates near blowed off that felt so good to leave behind, but the pain of livin' with all the fear and hurts we give each other."

"What about the others? Did you see them?"

"They were there too. The Wiggins boys were smilin' like they knew the funniest thing ever and even old four eyed Charlie Olsen had a grin on his face. They looked like kids that had been let out of school early. We all hung there just a smilin' at each other an' then somethin' or maybe someone told me I oughta look over by that waterin' trough. Next thing I knowed I was lookin' down on your half dead carcass thinkin' you was a gonna' float up to me. There for a little bit I seen you come out and you just hung there like somebody had picked you up by your coat collar, but you never completely opened your eyes, you just kinda' blinked once and then you sunk back down into yerself and moaned. I looked back toward the others and they was gone. I didn't know where they went or how to get there so I just stayed there a watchin' you sprawled out in the dirt. Without even thinkin' about it I hollered at ol' Marcus. He was startin' to dig a hole for my sorry remains and he flinched like he heard me. It was funny how he looked around kinda suspicious and went back to diggin'. I hollered again and told him to come over by the waterin' trough. He looked around an' decided he needed a drink anyhow so he moseyed over to the pump and spotted you layin' there so purty. He called the woman over and they looked at you fer a while an' she told him to haul what was left of you down here. I just been watchin' the show ever since. Seems like that's what I'm supposed to do. Actually it don't just *seem* like it, I know this is what I'm supposed to be a 'doin. That's the great thing about it, I really know that for once I'm a doin' what I'm supposed to do, even if I'm a little short on details."

One evening after supper Ike decided it was time to ask Mrs. Pendleton a question that had been on his mind. "Is there a possibility that I could send a letter to my wife? I would like to let her know that I am still alive. I just don't want her to despair."

The woman looked thoughtful. "Well, I can't just take it to the post office, but there may be other channels. I will not promise anything and I would expect to read your letter, but I will think about it." She was quiet after that and left shortly after this exchange.

Although he was never allowed out of the cellar, Ike heard comings and goings in the house over his head. He could hear footsteps in the room directly above, which he believed was the kitchen. He recognized Mrs. Pendleton's light tread and Marcus' heavier but still graceful footsteps. Other people came and went and Ike could hear voices but could not discern their conversations. He assumed that the callers were the reason he was kept in the cellar. According to Mrs. Pendleton the Home Guard kept watch over the neighborhood as much for Confederate deserters as for marauding Yankees.

"You think I could make it if I tried to escape?" Ike asked Johnny one day.

"I wondered if you were a gonna' be thinkin' about that. I ain't no fortune teller or nothin. Cain't see into the future, but I'd say it might be risky until you get to walkin' better. You'd look funny limpin' around Mississippi in that nightshirt."

As his leg improved and the pain in his head diminished, Ike walked back and forth across the cellar to exercise muscles that might otherwise have atrophied. Sometimes he would pick up one of the chairs and set it back down repeatedly to work his arms. When he was sufficiently healed he marched with his crutch on his shoulder and would stop and do maneuvers with it, it was not as heavy as his Springfield, but it helped him maintain his upper body strength. As he gained strength a nervous energy kept him moving like a trapped animal, he pictured a bear walking back and forth in the cage of the traveling circus he had seen once in his youth.

"You are kind of like a ol' bear Ikey. Lettin' your beard grow kinda' adds to the appearance too. Just don't get too growly."

Micheline Pendleton's son Todd had let his beard grow in competition with his fellow riders and his mother had decided that it was appropriate for Ike to let his beard grow as well. After a few days of itching he became comfortable with the beard and didn't miss the feel of Jasper Pendleton's razor on his skin. It crossed his mind that possibly Mrs. Pendleton didn't like the idea of his having control of a sharp object even if Marcus was supervising. He also wondered what Emma would think of him growing a beard.

As a result of his daily routine of walking and calisthenics Ike's strength improved, but it only added to his restlessness. He tested the door when things were quiet and found that it was secured with a wooden bar that slid into iron brackets at each end. He found it easy enough to raise the bar by sliding his butter knife between two boards and carefully lifting it at each end. Once he had the bar free of its attachments he carefully lifted the door. The bar slid off the side and clattered to the ground when the door was opened to a point where Ike could make it through. From his position the sound of the bar falling was thunderous. He looked over the edge of the door to see if his activity had been discovered. From somewhere to the far side of the house he could hear what sounded like someone chopping wood, he hoped it might be Marcus and that the noise of the axe had covered for the noise of the bar falling. Ike looked and listened, straining to hear any evidence that his attempt to escape had been noticed.

"Go on Ikey, I don' think they heard you." Johnny said in a breathless whisper.

"Why are you whispering?" Ike replied in his head in a similar manner.

"Force of habit, I guess. This is kinda' excitin' to me, you been pretty boring lately."

"I wonder where Mrs. Pendleton is." Ike thought.

"Maybe she's on the other side of the house puttin' posies on my grave." Johnny replied, still whispering, but giggling.

There were clothes on a line behind the house, clothes that could only be those of a very large man. Ike walked over and unpinned a pair of pants and a shirt that would have covered he and Johnny both. He was about to go behind the smokehouse to change into Marcus clothing when he spied the door of the cellar yawning at him, advertising that something was amiss. He eased the door and its bar back into position and then headed back to the smokehouse. Just as he was about to reach the cover of the building his bare foot found a sliver of broken glass that penetrated his right foot just far enough to send a bolt of pain up his leg. He stifled a scream and hopped on the other foot to the shade of the outbuilding and pulled out the glass. The cut wasn't too deep, and he had other things to concern himself with.

The shirt hung on Ike and the pants were not about to stay up on their own, he fashioned a crude gallus out of a piece of old rope he found and managed to hitch the pants up to a point where he could move and not lose them. Johnny was having a good deal of fun at Ike's expense as he tried to clothe himself. When he thought he was covered well enough, he peeked around the side of the smokehouse and still saw no one. His heart was beating so fast and hard that he could hear it in his ears as he gazed around and tried to decide on a plan of further action.

"When in doubt, head north!" Johnny said. With no better idea to counter with Ike did just that. He had positioned himself with the smokehouse between himself and the sound of the axe, which to his delight was still coming rhythmically. He darted to the east side of the house, which was the farthest from the chopping and still the axe blows came steadily. He ducked under a window as he eased along the side of the house and peered around the corner, only to find himself staring into the twin eyes of a double barreled shotgun. Mrs. Pendleton had no discernible expression as she walked Ike backwards over the last few yards he had gained in his quest for freedom.

"If you shoot me, Your son Todd may suffer for it!" Ike blurted out. He was suddenly angry and desperate to get the upper hand on the woman. They both came to a stop at the back corner of the house and she lowered the gun slightly.

"If I shoot you in the foot, he might just avoid combat or even get to come home early." She said pointing the gun at Ike's left foot. His own pulse pounded in his ears as she cocked the right hammer.

"Please don't, I'll go back down in the cellar!" Ike said, disgusted at the desperation in his own voice, but convinced that the woman would maim him for life.

"Ikey, she's bluffin', she won't shoot you, she think's she'll be hurtin' her boy!"

"How can you be so sure Johnny?" Ike responded in his mind. Before Johnny could respond the woman spoke again.

"If you manage to get away from here and get captured by the Confederates, they are likely to kill you for a spy or imprison you in a place where you could die of disease. If you get back to your own army, you would likely go right back to combat and you could get killed there. A few pieces of buckshot in your foot might not be so bad Mr. Lowery." She said sighting down the barrel at his foot. Ike closed his eyes and prayed.

"Ikey, she's bluffin' I'm tellin' you, do you see any percussion caps on that ol' shotgun?"

Just as Ike was opening his eyes to see if Johnny was right a pair of huge hands with a grip like a vise encircled his upper arms. "You don' look so good in my clothes dere sodjur." Marcus rumbled.

"Thank you Marcus, I didn't relish having to clean the buckshot out of his foot." Mrs. Pendleton said, easing the hammer down on her shotgun.

As Johnny had said there were no caps on the nipples of the shotgun, but it was too late for Ike to get away from Marcus. Ike was about to growl out that he had seen through the ruse, but Johnny urged him not to speak of it. "You shoulda' took my word for it, but I don't think you should let her know that you know it, just in case it happens again."

As Marcus was walking Ike back toward the cellar Micheline Pendleton let out a shriek that made Ike and his captor both jump. "Your right foot! You are bleeding from your right foot!" She wailed. Ike had forgotten having stepped on the glass, but he was bleeding enough to leave a trail.

"I stepped on a piece of glass I'm afraid." Ike said instinctively trying to express contrition.

Mrs. Pendleton stooped and examined the foot while Marcus easily lifted Ike off of the ground. When she was convinced that the damage was slight she stood up, faced Ike and slapped him with surprising force. "Don't ever do that again! Todd may well also have wounded himself. If he gets an infection and loses a foot….or worse, I will see to it that you suffer. Do you understand?"

Ike was angry now and glared at his assailant, which earned him another slap. Marcus moved Ike away from Mrs. Pendleton before she could slap him again. It was a bitter relief to be returned to the cellar.

"Good going there Ikey, you turned the other cheek for sure." Johnny chuckled, "She slapped you so hard, I even kinda' felt it."

Marcus was gentle but insistent as he shepherded his charge down the stairs. He handed Ike the night shirt that had been abandoned by the smokehouse and retrieved his own clothing. Ike was given soap, water, a linen cloth, and some ointment to put on his wounded foot. No supper was delivered that evening and it was several days before Mrs. Pendleton returned to his quarters.

A weight of some sort was added to the door. Ike tested the new obstacle by displacing the bar with his butter knife again but the weight was far too much for him to budge. After a few attempts at heaving the door open with his shoulder Ike gave it up. He went back to reading until he realized that he had left the bar out of position. Terror of his latest attempt at escape being discovered made him shiver and he did so until he was able to slide the bar back down with the knife.

Squinting through the knothole and the crack in the door gave him little view of the outside world and its goings on. He would try to catch glimpses when the door was held open, but Marcus filled the opening nearly completely as he entered or exited and he didn't feel it was proper to try to peer around Mrs. Pendleton on the rare occasions that she visited him in the daytime.

One evening as Ike was reading from the light of his candle lamp there were loud voices in the house above. Heavy footsteps and a scuffle overhead disturbed his reading of Alexandre Dumas. He had been engrossed in the man's novels and was feeling a kinship with "The Man in the Iron Mask."

"What's going on Johnny?" He said, unconcerned about how connected he had become with his invisible companion.

"Momma Pendleton has company, and I don't think they was invited. Sit still now and let's see what happens. You might just want to put that light out."

Ike put down the book and blew out his candle without questioning Johnny. Men were shouting and tromping around in the kitchen above his head and he heard Micheline Pendleton voice retorting in anger.

"Old gal sounds like a wildcat when she's mad don't she Ikey. I guess you know that though." Johnny said, again in his stage whisper.

"I wonder where Marcus is."

"Don't know, I cain't see through that floor any better than you can, but somehow I think Marcus is out of the picture for a while. If he was up and around he'd be right in the middle of that and those fellers would be a gettin' clobbered."

The scuffling footsteps exited the kitchen and Ike heard the noise approaching the door to his abode. Instinctively he grabbed his crutch and crouched in the corner under the steps where he wouldn't likely be seen when the door opened.

"Let's just see what you got down there in that cellar where your darky is always goin'" came a voice from outside. "Hold still there you bitch!" was followed by a loud slap and a moan from the woman.

Ike heard a savage grunt heard as the weight was slid off the door. The bar was roughly slid from its brackets and clattered on the ground. Lantern light brightened the interior of what had been Ike's comfortable world only minutes earlier, but left its occupant in shadow in his corner under the steps. A small figure in a filthy Union uniform came down the steps with the lamp. The man stared at the bed and the table and chairs and called back up the steps to someone else. "George, I don't see any silver or gold but you need to see this. I think I know what she's been doin' down here with her Nigger." The man took a swig from a bottle he carried with him. Ike recognized the smell of Jasper Pendleton's brandy.

Ike kept his back to the wall and just out of the light. He could see most of what was going on by peering between the steps. The man with the lantern appeared to be a deserter. The intruder was fixated on the unmade bed and his fantasy of its purpose and didn't look around. Ike grasped the shaft of his crutch like a club when the man backed up beside the stairway to make room for his partner, who was carrying Mrs. Pendleton down the steps. The man had backed up uncomfortably close and Ike was in no position to get a good swing.

"Hold on Ikey, hold on a bit." Johnny cautioned. His voice still came as a stage whisper and had the breathless quality of someone watching a cockfight.

Another shabby man in the remains of a blue uniform came down the steps dragging the woman by her waist with one arm. He had her arms pinioned behind her with his other hand. She looked around wildly, glimpsing Ike but not looking in his direction. She dropped her head to her breast and sobbed loudly, keeping the men's attention on her.

"Looks like she has her valuable's hid away somewhere else, but maybe if we're real nice to her she might just fall in love with one of us and show us where they might be, reckon Teddy?"

George threw Mrs. Pendleton down on the bed and stood over her breathing heavily. "I might not be as well fixed as that big buck of yours old gal, but I reckon I'll have me as good a time as he ever had. Maybe even better.

Let's get them fine clothes off you and see some of your other treasures."

"You'll pay for this when you are caught!" The woman rasped.

"We got so much to pay for if either side catches us that what we do to you really don't matter much at all." George chuckled "We don't plan on gettin' caught anyway, we're gonna' get away from here when we're done with you and head west and ride out this war."

The woman screamed as George tore at her blouse. Ike was still cramped up in the corner unsure of the best way to proceed. Teddy was standing so close to him that he could barely move without touching him and giving himself away.

"Now if you could get that crutch over Teddy's head and up agin' his windpipe you could choke the life out of him with him between you and George." Johnny's voice came in a hoarse whisper. "With any luck he might drop that lantern and put the light out so George won't know what's happeninin'. Just be patient Ikey, he'll move forward to get a look at her titties any minute now and you can get in a better position. Now don't you be peekin' yerself." Johnny giggled.

Just as Johnny predicted Teddy crept towards the bed as his companion ripped the bodice off the sobbing woman. "She looks pretty good for her age don't she George. I'll be glad to watch while you go first and get her warmed up for me." Teddy took one more pull on the brandy and re-corked it. He set the bottle down on the table, wiped his mouth with his sleeve, and concentrated his efforts on watching every detail of the performance.

The woman tried to rise up and resist her attacker as he was undoing his belt and dropping his filthy pants. He backhanded her and put his right hand to her throat. "Keep it up old girl, I kinda like a little feistiness." he said as he ripped her skirt and underclothing piece by piece from her body.

"You mighta' avoided this if you'd told us where you hid your goods but since you didn't this is what you get." George said, breathing hard with excitement. "Now think about this while we're havin' our fun old gal. If you don't tell us after that we're just gonna burn this place down with you in it. Maybe a good pokin' will help your memory."

Ike had been frightened and unsure of how to proceed up to that moment. Part of him wanted to watch the woman's degradation and let her suffer. George's threat of fire sent Ike into a rage. The image of flames from his dream reappeared so strongly that he nearly forgot himself and his situation and moaned from the heat. When the vision passed Ike knew Johnny's idea would work and he prepared himself to see it through.

Teddy inched forward a little more and Ike saw his chance. The little man was breathing heavily and was intent on watching their victim's defilement. "Come on George, show her how a Yankee does it." He said, holding the lamp in one hand and his own crotch with the other.

Just as Ike moved out from under the stairs and whipped the crutch around the smaller man's neck a puff of what felt like a cool breeze blew out the fire in the lantern in the instant before it fell to the floor. The shaft of the crutch choked off Teddy's air and he wasn't able to make much more than a nasal whimper, his hands came up and fluttered at the shaft of the crutch on either side of his neck but he didn't have the strength to overcome his attacker. The little man was scrawny to begin with and too drunk on Jasper Pendleton's brandy to resist much. The reek from Teddy's long unwashed body was nauseating and added to Ike's resolve. Ike's arm muscles were strong from weeks of nervous exercise and he easily crushed the struggling man's windpipe. When Teddy's body relaxed a quick jerk from Ike snapped his neck vertebrae. The fresh corpse jittered briefly and then went limp with only the crutch supporting it.

George had grunted in surprise when darkness enveloped him. "Teddy, what are you doin'..... where's the light? Teddy...Teddy...Teddy!" He whined his accomplice's name more feebly with each repetition.

Once Ike felt the resistance leave Teddy he shifted to his right and dropped his lifeless body to the floor, where it would no longer be between him and his next quarry. Clouds had been obscuring the moon but they parted momentarily and a shaft of moonlight came through the open door and illuminated George as he started to rise from the bed where his victim lay panting.

"Who, who's there?" he croaked just before Micheline Pendleton's knee contacted his crotch with as much force as she could muster. The man's high pitched squeal ended abruptly as the heavy end of Ike's crutch connected with his skull, shattering the back of it and shoving bits of bone and fragments of wood into George's brain. He fell forward onto the woman and the front of his head thumped hers and knocked her senseless.

Ike stood in the ray of moonlight panting.

"Boy Ikey, you're a regular panther when you get your blood up. I figured you was rusty at fightin' after bein' down here for so long. You killed both of them fellers."

"You sure?"

"If there's anythin' I know for sure these days it's who's dead. I saw em come out a lookin' all confused an' sorry like. I couldn't help myself an' I hollered "Boo!" and they both skedaddled to I don't know where, maybe I don't want to know...... but they sure are dead. If they ever was a pair that needed killin' I think they was. Good thing you don't need that crutch anymore 'cause you broke the head clean off of it.

"Johnny......I didn't mean to kill them, I just wanted to keep them from hurting her any more....I just wanted to stop them from burning......"

"Well you stopped em for good Ike, but you didn't have a lot of choice, they woulda killed her after they had their way with her a time or two and if they had seen you they wouldn't have let you live either. I'm afraid they might have done away with old Marcus."

A sudden realization washed over Ike, for the first time since he had been carried down to this cellar there was no door or no large black man between him and freedom. He looked up the steps through the open door and at the moon that seemed to be staring down at him, asking him to come out. He loped to the top of the stairs and reveled in being free of the cellar for the first time in months. He was free! Looking back down the stairs he saw Mrs. Pendleton form lying defenseless on his bed, with a dead man on top of her.

"No, you know you can't leave her here like this Ikey, you gotta' help her. You don't know who else might be hangin' around out there."

"Johnny, this is my chance, I need to get out of here. I saved her life, isn't that enough?" Ike said out loud. He stood there a few moments staring up at the moon and looked back down the steps at the woman. George's head was on her shoulder as if they had both went to sleep in passionate embrace. He would at least have to get the man's body off of her.

"I suppose you're right Johnny." Ike replied with a sigh.

"Of course I'm right. Now settle down a little bit and let's see if you can carry that poor ol' gal back up stairs. Maybe you oughta' wrap somethin' around her for modesty's sake. Now don't go pokin' or grabbin' anything. I gotta admit Teddy was right, she does look pretty good yet."

"Johnny, would you quit chattering like a squirrel." Ike said out loud forgetting himself again.

"Did you notice how the lantern went out Ikey? I did that, somehow I managed to make me a little wind and blew it out so it wouldn't set fire to everthin." Johnny crowed.

"You always were full of wind, I think you've gotten worse since you died."

He dragged George's heavy body off the unconscious woman and carefully wrapped her in his bed sheet and quilt. He was anxious to cover her as soon as possible, seeing her like this aroused him in spite of himself. He felt guilty for his reaction and embarrassed that she would know he had seen her like this. The moonlight was sufficient for him to see as he carried her up the steps. He blinked and looked around to get his bearings. She was light and Ike had recuperated his strength to the point that she was easy to carry, but the feel of her body so close to his made him uncomfortable and he was eager to unburden himself of her. Light from the kitchen window illuminated the back steps and he carried her into the house.

There was a day bed in the kitchen and Ike laid his burden on it. One shapely breast fell out from the tangle of bedclothes and Ike quickly rearranged her coverings with as much propriety as he possibly could.

"You're a good boy Ikey, back in the day I probably would have had to give that a squeeze." Johnny chortled.

"Well, I've got my guardian angel here with me so I have to behave now don't I."

"Wonder what happened to old Marcus?" Johnny mused. "Maybe he's not dead, I don't see no big black ghost wanderin' around anywhere. He'd have to come round and see 'bout "Missy"."

Ike looked around the house and found a stairway. The thought occurred to him that if there were night clothes that fit him there might be other clothes as well. At the top of the stairs was a bedroom with no bed. Thinking this must be Todd's room he rummaged through a chest and found the items he needed. Everything fit well and before long he was clad in plain but well made clothing including underwear and boots that fit him perfectly. He found his old uniform in one of Todd's drawers, it appeared to have been cleaned and repaired. It didn't seem like a good idea to be wearing a Union uniform this evening, so he left it where it was. He wondered why she had kept it.

"Maybe she thought she might have to bury you in it." Johnny chortled as Ike headed back down the stairs.

"Looks like you got you some travelin' clothes Ikey." Johnny chuckled. "Good idea even if you stole 'em."

"I didn't steal them Johnny, I traded my uniform for them." Ike replied sending Johnny into a gale of laughter. "They definitely fit me better than Marcus's clothes too." He thought briefly that if he were caught in civilian clothes he could be taken for a spy and hanged, but wearing a uniform still seemed to be the worse of his options. Todd Pendleton's clothing was less scratchy than the wool of Ike's uniform and might be less conspicuous.

Mrs. Pendleton was still unconscious but breathing steadily. She had a knot rising on her forehead where George's head had hit hers.

Ike was pondering what to do next when he heard a noise in the back yard that sounded like a cow bellowing. Looking out he saw a pitiful figure making its way to the house.

Marcus was crawling toward the back steps on his hands and knees. Blood dripped from a gash in his forehead but he was moving toward his mistress as if drawn by a magnet. "Missy.... Missy....... where is she?" he sobbed.

The big man's anguish was pitiful to see. It was all Ike could do to get the overwrought giant to his feet and walk him up the steps into the kitchen. Once he saw his mistress and determined that she was still alive he relaxed and sat heavily in a chair to keep vigil over her.

Ike took charge of Marcus and cleaned the gash in his forehead as the big man sat as if in a daze, ever watching Mrs. Pendleton as if she might disappear at any moment. "He looks like a stunned ox." Johnny said in wonder. "Big as a young one, I 'spect a normal man would be dead by now." Ike found some salve that smelled like what Marcus had put on his own forehead and returned the favor before bandaging the silent man's head. Ike edged toward the back door and stood looking out at the moon, thinking that now might be his chance to leave when Micheline Pendleton began to stir.

She blinked a few times and looked at the two men who were staring at her. The situation registered in her mind after a few moments and she looked down in horror at her state of dress. She sat up primly, carefully keeping the bed clothes drawn around her.

"Marcus, can you talk?" she said, looking at her servant with concern. She moved close to him and put her hand on his arm. The big man had been looking down as if in shame. At her touch he looked up and made eye contact. Micheline Pendleton smiled warmly when their eyes met, eliciting a look of relief and adoration from the wounded man.

"Hey Ikey, while them two's a comfortin' each other don't you think you might be getting' outta' here?" Johnny said in his stage whisper.

Ike moved quietly toward the door, but turned back to catch the exchange between Mrs. Pendleton and Marcus.

"I'm just restin' a spell Missy. Feel better now that you'se alright. Don't quite know what happened, somebody hit me in the head with a shovel I thinks."

"There were two of them, I was afraid they might have killed you, they tried to take advantage of me in the cellar, but Mr. Lowery ......" she said trailing off and turning to Ike, who had been forgotten for a few moments and who was standing at the back door looking out at the moon and trying to decide which direction to run. "Did you kill them?"

"I'm afraid so, I may have gotten carried away, but I don't think there was a lot of choice." He hesitated, thinking this was the time he should be bounding out the door. Marcus and Mrs. Pendleton were well enough to take care of each other and he didn't think Marcus would be up to pursuing him just yet.

Hoof beats in the yard interrupted their conversation. "Get under the bed, quick!" Mrs. Pendleton ordered Ike, "Stay here Marcus, I'll handle this." She took one quick look to make sure Ike was hidden before she readjusted the bedclothes she was wrapped in and headed for the front of the house.

There was a frantic knock on the door as the woman gathered herself and walked to the front door with as much dignity as she could manage under the circumstances. When she opened the door a man's voice could be heard. "My God, Micheline what happened to you?"

"I'm so glad you came Colonel, I have been attacked in my own home, it was awful. There were two of them, Yankee deserters I think. My man Marcus managed to chase them off."

"It must have been the same two that the home guard spotted early this morning, we thought they might have come this way. I'm so sorry we didn't get here sooner to spare you. I hope they didn't......?"

"They attempted to assault me, yes. They were looking for valuables and when they didn't find anything else that suited them they tried to have their way with me. Brave Marcus caught them and beat them badly and they ran away in the direction of the swamp. I can only hope they fall into it and drown. One of them fetched Marcus a blow to the head, but he will recover shortly I believe."

"Can I see him?"

"He's back in the kitchen, do come in. I bound his wound, which was minor for a man of his strength."

Ike heard the tromping of a big man's feet coming down the hall. He plastered himself to the wall under the day bed and tried not to breathe. He watched the muddy cavalry boots approach and stop next to the chair where Marcus was slumped. Micheline Pendleton's feet followed, she was still wearing the shoes that were about all her attacker had left on her body. Her feet seemed to move about nervously as the Colonel began to speak. Ike realized that she was as frightened as he was. While she was not likely to be shot, hanged, or imprisoned if her account of the evening were to be discovered as the fiction that it was, she was still bent on keeping Ike's presence a secret.

"Marcus you big rascal, sounds like you've had a hard night. Did you get a good look at them?"

"Jus' like Missy said.... couple.... boys in blue. She can 'scribe 'em better....kinda hurts to talk Colonel, one hit me in 'da jaw." Marcus mumbled theatrically. Ike heard the scratching as he rubbed his massive jowl.

To his horror Ike noticed the muddy tracks coming in the back door, one set led directly to where he lay trapped. If the Colonel saw the line of mud leading under the day bed that indicated Ike's presence there he didn't acknowledge it. He kept staring at the muddy tracks as Mrs. Pendleton described George and Teddy.

"Those are likely the two that murdered our boys earlier. I think we'd better take off after them, maybe we can catch them yet. I'll post a few of my men around your place this evening Micheline, in case they come back. These are cowardly but dangerous men, they killed a couple of our home guard, just young boys on picket, cut their throats before they could make a sound. It was bad enough when the damned Yankees came down here and invaded us, then they started stealing from the populace, and now that we have pushed them out we have their dregs to deal with."

One of the "dregs" was developing a cramp in his leg from being crammed in under the day bed in the Pendleton's kitchen. Ike gritted his teeth so hard that he thought the grinding noise would give him away and earn him a painful death or imprisonment.

"Are you alright Micheline?" the Colonel asked. "You don't look well."

"I will be fine Colonel, it has just been a very stressful evening."

"Frankly, I have been worried about you staying out here by yourself since Jasper died. I'm glad you have Marcus, but I wish we had enough men to keep someone out here all the time."

"I appreciate your concern Colonel, but we will be fine, as you can see, Marcus can handle about any situation." The woman said. Ike was afraid he would pass out from the pain and moan out loud when the Colonel finally left the kitchen. He distracted himself by thinking what might have happened had he escaped out the back door. Chances are he would have been caught by the Colonel and his men and he might well have been killed or at least imprisoned.

After the Colonel took his leave Ike crawled out from under the bed. He stood and stretched and massaged the muscles in his leg. Marcus was still sitting in the chair looking mournful. "Gettin' old, let them two get the best of me and they hurt Missy. I thanks you for what you did." He looked toward the stairs where his mistress had retreated to dress herself properly. "Don't know what I do if anything happened to Missy."

"He sure looks after that woman don't he Ikey. Wonder what that's all about? Guess tonight ain't so good for you gettin' away from here."

Mrs. Pendleton stepped into the room and stared at Ike in his purloined clothing. "Were you planning on going somewhere Mr. Lowery?"

"It had crossed my mind. Not knowing what else might be required of me this evening I thought it might be a good idea to be dressed in something other than that nightshirt." He met her gaze and tried to remain expressionless. Tension hung in the room like a fog. "It looks like we have some problems here, at least two down in the cellar, with the house being guarded it will be difficult to dispose of them discreetly."

"Moon be a settin' in about a hour." Marcus said, breaking the silence. "They's that ol' dried up well behind the barn. Some quicklime and dirt take care of they carcasses."

"Can we get them out there without being seen or heard, Marcus?" Ike asked, relieved at the thought of a solution.

"I go walk around and see where them boys posted befo' the moon sets." Marcus said, standing up slowly. "Head's feelin' better now. Thanks sodjur."

With Marcus outside determining where the Colonel had placed his pickets, Ike and the woman resumed their challenging stares. Neither spoke or even blinked for a few minutes. "Can't read her mind Ikey, but I think she'd like to get you back down in the cellar."

"At this point Johnny, it might be the best place for me. If I try to get away and get caught by the home guard or the cavalry about the best I could hope for is to be shot on sight. Their blood's up and I can't entirely blame them. I'm the one that went crazy and killed those two for assaulting the flower of southern womanhood and I'm a damned Yankee."

Mrs. Pendleton finally looked away, tired by her evening's travails and not being able to gain an advantage in the contest. Ike stood up and walked toward her peering at the knot on her forehead.

"Shouldn't we put something on that?" he offered. When she did not respond, he went to the cabinet and retrieved the salve. He led her to a chair and helped her sit down. She did not resist as he knelt beside her and cleaned the abrasion on her forehead and applied the balm tenderly. When she finally turned to look at him there were tears in her eyes.

"I am afraid that I have treated you badly Mr. Lowery. Thank you for all you've done this evening. It's likely that you saved my life." She said putting her head on his shoulder and began sobbing, "This war has been so ugly and taken so much from so many."

They remained there in silence Ike instinctively put his arm around the woman's shoulder as she clung to him and vented her pent up sadness. Marcus stepped into the kitchen and registered no surprise or dismay at the scene. "Nobody anywhere close to the well and the moon behind a cloudbank. We better do this thing now if we gonna' do it."

"Marcus, is there any chance we could get them into the creek behind the barn so they could float away and maybe be found?" Ike asked, mentally picturing the landscape he had seen when his squad first reconnoitered the area.

Marcus looked thoughtful for a moment. "Creek is up right now and everthin's in shadow, ain't but about 'nother fitty' yard. Dat way iff'n the 'Federts find 'em they be settlin' down a while an' won't be lookin' around so much. Good idea dere sodjur."

Teddy was the lighter of the two dead men and had only voided his bladder at the moment of his demise. George on the other hand was heavy even after having evacuated nearly all of his internal contents as well as bleeding from his head wound. "It's going to stink down here for days." Ike groaned in disgust as he and Marcus rolled the dead man's mortal remains onto an old piece of canvas and carried him up the steps and onto a wheelbarrow. Ike shed his borrowed clothing and floated the dead men out to the center of the stream and sent them on their way

"Ashes to ashes, dust to dust, if the good Lord don't want 'em, the devil must." Johnny intoned as the corpses drifted away.

"That's very angelic Johnny." Ike replied, thinking of all the men he had killed in the last two years. These two had worn the same uniform as he and his comrades but their deaths were less troubling to him than a number of the enemy that he had seen crumple to the ground when he shot them. These two men's demise had been close at hand and he had stopped them from the commission of rape, multiple murder, and arson. Still he wondered if these two had families somewhere. It was possible that one or both of these miscreants had people who would always wonder what had happened to them. He had seen no identification on either one of them, but he hadn't searched them thoroughly either.   It had crossed his mind to try to purloin any knife or other weapon that might be on the men's bodies, but Marcus had been too close to make that a possibility. The thought of using a weapon against Marcus was abhorrent to him anyway. He went in to the barn to put his clothing back on. The moon peeked out from behind the cloudbank for a few minutes before it sat behind the trees. The pale light reflected on the water and illuminated the wake of George and Teddy's last journey.

Marcus said little as he and Ike went about cleaning up the cellar and erasing the traces of the two intruders. "See ya' in da mawnin'" he finally said as he went up the steps for the last time and closed the door. Ike heard the bar and the stone being replaced as usual. He also saw the brandy bottle sitting on the table. He stared at it for a few moments, and then changed back into his nightshirt which had been returned to him, and blew out the candle and went to bed.

"That bottle is a callin' you ain't it Ikey." Johnny intoned. "You're wantin' more than just a nightcap."

"Yes, Johnny it's tempting me, but I think I can get through this without it. Some people can handle the beast, and some can't. It's never brought me anything but grief."

Ike turned his back on the bottle that he could not see but whose presence he could feel. He prayed fervently for the strength to resist a temptation that had gotten the best of him so many times before. Johnny's voice was silent as Ike prayed. After a time, he slept and dreamed of home for a while. Then his dreams turned to loss and death and flames. The violence of the previous evening was revisited as he once again witnessed George and Teddy dragging Micheline Pendleton down to his abode. Scenes of other violent events swam through his mind, he saw the first man he had killed jerk with the impact of the bullet and crumple to the ground and felt the horror that had frozen him in his tracks until Jimmy had grabbed him and drug him back into the retreating line of soldiers. Once again he was in the cellar as two Union Soldiers drug Mrs. Pendleton down the steps. This time it was Ike and Johnny laughing and abusing the woman as she fought and sobbed. He awoke to the screams of a woman dying as her house burned down around her. He listened intently to make sure that the screaming was not for real, but only heard the ringing in his own ears.

It was a couple of hours before dawn and Ike's bladder kept him from rolling over and going back to sleep. He still remembered some of the dream and thought it was a shadow from the fear he had felt when George had threatened to burn down this house that had become his home or his prison. He felt his way to the chamber pot and sweet relief. His fingers brushed the bottle as he passed the table on his way back to bed. "Ikey........" Johnny warned, but the desire for the brandy crowded out all his warnings.

A short swig turned into another longer one. The first small burst of warmth fanned the flames of Ike's desire for the feeling of detachment and separation from the pain of living that he had always found in alcohol. There was not enough brandy left to give Ike the release he sought. "Nothin' good woulda' come from this old friend." Johnny intoned, his voice sounding more like an echo.

"Shut up you red headed bastard! I don't want to hear you anymore! You aren't for real, I'm just sick in the head and making you up. I wish there was enough brandy to make you go away. Why won't you leave me alone!" Ike said out loud as he dashed the now empty bottle against the stone wall by the chamber pot and fell into Todd Pendleton's feather bed. He dreamed again of a conflagration, this time he thought he might be glimpsing Hell.

He was walking unsteadily down a street that felt familiar even though he couldn't place where it was or why he would know of it. Thunder had muttered at first and then gained in volume and frequency as lightning flashed and lit up the surroundings. Shabby houses sat close to the dirt and gravel track that could only be called a street with some generosity and would soon be a mire of mud as the rain started in earnest. The earth shook as a bolt struck so close that the white of it nearly blinded him. He smelled the smoke first and then saw the flames. He was drawn toward an orange glow at the end of the street. People were coming out of their houses as they watched the fire. The first Rebel soldier that he had killed that first morning at Pittsburgh Landing stood gaping at the fire. A hole in the man's chest oozed blood in small rhythmic spurts, pumped by a heart that should have long ago stopped beating. George and Teddy stood pointing at the house and laughing and passed a bottle of Jasper Pendleton's brandy back and forth. The structure looked like the Pendleton house at first and then it shifted and became a smaller somehow familiar house as it was consumed. Ike staggered and then ran as if his life depended on it. The fire that could only have been a block away seemed to recede. He ran like a man possessed but his progress toward the fire was slow, his legs and lungs ached as if he had run for hours. A skeletal hand grabbed his right ankle and stopped him in his tracks briefly. Looking down Ike saw the corpse that he and Johnny had been dragging to the burial trench in his previous dream. He dragged the corpse for several yards until the rotting fingers separated from the hand and scattered along the road. Pain from the intense heat of the burning structure soon surpassed that of his limbs and breathing apparatus as he finally drew near the conflagration. He put his hands up to shield his face from the fire but he couldn't help himself, someone was in that house and he had to save them. Just as he was about to plunge into the fire other hands grabbed him and dragged him back, his clothing smoking.

Chapter 3 – The Epistle

For the next two days Marcus brought breakfast before daylight and supper well after dark, lunch was included on the breakfast tray. Ike assumed that traffic to and from the cellar was minimized to avoid drawing attention to his abode. The only comment made about the broken bottle as the shards were swept up and removed was when Marcus shook his head and said "Jasper's last bottle of 'Poleon brandy."

Johnny's voice was no longer present. Ike felt relieved, believing that it was a sign that he was recovering both his health and his sanity. His memory was still in shambles, but the absence of Johnny's running commentary gave him hope that they might return on their own.

The third day after the attack Ike heard hoof beats in the yard and booted footsteps in the kitchen above. He sat still and prayed that his presence would remain a secret, as troubling as his situation was; he wasn't ready to be a prisoner of the confederacy. Marcus informed him later that the home guard had discovered what was left of George and Teddy a mile down the creek. The guard around the house was lifted and Marcus and his mistress could move about more freely. Ike knew that this freedom did not apply to him.

The fourth evening after the incident, Mrs. Pendleton herself came with the evening meal. She had gone to great lengths to prepare the food. There was crisp fried chicken, biscuits, potatoes, and greens fried with bacon and onions and apple pie that was still warm.

The abrasion and bruise on Mrs. Pendleton's forehead was fading and had been powdered carefully to further conceal it. She smiled at Ike and asked about his well being. After they had eaten she gave Ike the small package he had been eying since she came down to his domicile. He unwrapped his gift and find several sheets of what looked to be very expensive stationary, an envelope, a pen, and a small bottle of ink.

"I have decided to fulfill your request to send a letter to your wife. I can imagine the joy it will bring her and your families to know that you are still alive. I know too well how it feels to have lost someone you love. Marcus can get your letter into the hands of one of the slaves that are continually slinking away and going north. It was his idea actually, but I agree that you have earned our gratitude and this is some small thing we can do. I do intend to read the letter and I do not expect you to be sending a message to the military revealing your situation."

"That's fine Ma'am. I appreciate that this might be difficult for you. It will be a comfort to Emma to know that I am still alive even if I can't divulge the complete circumstances." Ike said and decided to change the subject. "You're looking well, I'm glad to see you recovering. I know it must have been awful for you."

"Yes it was Mr. Lowery, but I believe the incident is just one more sign that you were sent here for a purpose. If you hadn't been here, I might very well have been killed after suffering greatly from those beasts. You even kept the balance when you killed those two awful men. The two dead Yankees for the two poor youngsters they slaughtered. I have prayed long on these matters and am reassured you are here as a counterbalance for Todd. You and he are linked together.....do you see it?"

"I....suppose so. In some way there is a connection." Ike replied with caution wondering just how many others George and Teddy must have killed. Part of him wanted to bring that to her attention, but he decided to wait until his letter had been written and delivered first.

"But can you not feel it, Mr. Lowery?" she said breathlessly, leaning toward him and searching his face as if she was looking for a sign.

For a moment Ike found himself wondering if there was really something to the woman's delusion. After all, he was the one who had spent months in conversation with someone who wasn't really there. Was her delusion any less believable?

As a way to change the subject Ike thought of a question he had been meaning to ask one of his captors. "What day is it? I am used to putting a date on correspondence and I have lost track of time since I have been here."

Mrs. Pendleton had to think for a moment herself. "Wednesday, November 18 I believe." She looked to Marcus for confirmation.

"Yas'm." Marcus intoned.

The following day Ike devoted himself to writing his letter. He felt at a loss for words for a while and prayed for guidance. He found himself missing Johnny and his interjections. Finally the words started to come. He wrote them down as if he were in a trance. He had much he wanted to say, but didn't want Mrs. Pendleton to have the satisfaction of seeing too far into his private life. He paid close attention to his handwriting and made sure not to let the pen drip and make blotches on this treasured missal. He was restrained in his expressions due to the knowledge that Micheline Pendleton would be reading every word. He let the ink dry, read it over one more time, folded the letter neatly and placed it in the envelope, which he had addressed so carefully. He sat staring at the address and thinking of home and the reaction the letter would cause. Try as he might, there were details of his life that he could not bring to mind. The message seemed too short and sterile to him, but he could think of nothing else to add. He wondered if the letter would really find its way North.

He read it over one last time. It seemed like a letter written by someone else, but it was the best he felt that he could do in his circumstances. He was reaching out to the one person he loved most in this world, but it seemed like she was in some other world so far from him. He pictured Emma's expression when she drew the letter from its envelope. He held the treasured message in his hand and prayed that its words would bring comfort and hope. Try as he might he could not remember much of what he wrote after he put it in the envelope, he drew it out once more and read it.

Thursday, November 19, 1863

Dearest Emma,

Yes, I am still very much alive. I would expect by now that you might have heard that I was killed in a skirmish. While I was lost to my regiment and suffered a minor wound, I have had the good fortune to be rescued by others and while I can't divulge the details, I am held captive by a more benign element of the confederacy and will be until the war ends, which I pray will be soon. I am being well cared for and my health is improving. My only suffering is that I am separated from you and our loved ones. I think of you constantly and pray that this letter finds you in good health.

Please relieve the anxiety of both our families by letting them know of my survival and robust health. I particularly want you to convey my thoughts to my poor aged Father. When he and I last parted company there was much unpleasantness, and while I am sorry for my part in it and have the greatest respect and affection for him my position has not changed. I look forward to seeing him again and amiably working out our differences. I fondly anticipate shaking his trembling old hand once more in friendship before he passes on.

Dearest one, my happiest memories are of time spent with you in our home. I often picture you on our porch with dear Freddy at your feet guarding you and our home with his characteristic loyalty. I dream of the time when I will walk back into our yard to see his noble head rise from his paws in recognition. I think often of our desire to start a family and pray we can do so in a more peaceful country, my circumstances for now give me time to reflect on how important family is and what a wonderful mother you will be.

Please pray for me, that I will have the strength to endure my exile. I pray that you will take comfort in knowing that the worst part of this ordeal is my separation from you. You are always in my most fervent of prayers and the anticipation of seeing you again is what makes this life endurable.

Your loving Husband,

Ike

Mrs. Pendleton read the letter that evening after supper and nodded approvingly. She stared at Ike for a long time. "I believe

Marcus will get this into capable hands. He knows how to do many things well. I do not know what I would do without him." She said looking distant.

"I take it that Marcus has been with you for a long time." Ike said, trying not to seem as if he was prying.

"Marcus has looked out for me since I was a baby. He came with me here when Jasper and I married and looked after my sons as if they were his own."

"Do you ever worry that he might run away?"

"You people from the north just don't understand our Negroes. Marcus has always been more than just property, he is family. He will not leave me. He has had papers that said he was a free man for years, he was never technically a slave, but he insists on staying."

Ike thought of the many slaves who had greeted the Union army as their liberators. He had heard stories of mistreatment that rivaled those in "Uncle Tom's Cabin". What he heard the most was the simple desire of human beings to direct their own lives. He supposed that in his own way Marcus was using his freedom in the way he wished.

Life in the cellar returned to a routine of sleeping, exercising, eating, and reading. Ike looked longingly at the sky through the knothole in the cellar door. Mrs. Pendleton had informed him that the confederacy was still in control of this part of Mississippi and that the home guard kept a close watch on the area around her farm. He had been allowed to keep the clothing he took from Todd's room on the night of the attack and wore it during the daytime as the weather became cooler.

Ike could hear the chimes of the clock in the kitchen above him. He had seen the clock when he was in the kitchen on the night of the attack and it reminded him of the clock that Emma had brought with her when they were married. He had paid attention to when the clock stuck and on sunny days he scratched marks on the first wooden step with the tines of his fork that marked the position of the bar of light from the crack in the door to correspond with the hours. Within days of his imprisonment he had improvised a primitive sundial and could tell the approximate time by the location of the beam. His treasured pocket watch had been damaged when he had plunged into a creek on a foray to try to find a short route to Corinth, Mississippi a few days before the attack at Pittsburgh Landing. He had mailed the watch back home in hopes that he could one day have it repaired. Emma had often chided him for being so obsessed with knowing what time it was. Time seemed to stand still sometimes during his stay in Mrs. Pendleton's cellar and seeing the hours progress was reassuring. He told himself that every hour brought him closer to freedom.

He used one of the remaining sheets of writing paper to make a calendar. It had been May the 20th when Ike had first set foot on Micheline Pendleton's property. He had spent six months of his life in this cellar. This was the longest span of time he had spent in one place since his childhood, and as it had been in childhood, the days seemed to stretch out forever. Having a calendar might make it seem longer, but something in Ike always wanted to know what time it was, and what day.

On clear nights he watched the stars through his small private portal. Orion strode across the sky in pursuit of game. The old hunter's endless search reminded Ike of how he and his brother had watched the sky with their Pa when they were children. He hadn't thought of Jimmy much since he had been in the cellar, and still could not remember his face or many details of their childhood, but seeing the same stars they had loved to watch as children brought back a lost memory of their childhood and re-opened the wound that had been gouged in his soul when Jimmy died back at Shiloh. Loneliness nearly overwhelmed him as he looked at that night sky. He mourned the loss of his brother and for the first time he was able to begin to mourn the loss of Johnny, who had become like a brother to him.

Ike sat looking up at the sky and thought back to the day Jimmy died. His brother's face became more distinct to him as he recalled the last day he saw it.

The camp was just coming to life that morning. Bacon was frying, coffee was boiling, men were complaining about all the little things there are to complain about when you spend the night in the open with only a ground cloth and a wool blanket between your body and the ground. They had been ordered into line back on Friday and had stood, sat, or lain on the ground to sleep a little since then. Their pickets had been hearing noises and seeing movement in the woods and had claimed to have exchanged fire with Rebels just to their front. Ike would rather spend the day drilling and watching the woods and fields of Tennessee come to life as spring brought about its countless miracles than to remain in line waiting for an enemy that General Sherman and the rest of the high command seemed to believe was not there.

Ike had been to the latrine trench and was walking back to camp. Johnny had just stood up and was scratching his behind when they heard noises to their front. At first it sounded like children with firecrackers. One or two pops were followed by a sound like a large string had been set off. Then there was a ripping sound like someone was tearing heavy cloth. Then came the long roll of the regimental drum. Men grabbed their clothing, cartridge boxes and other things they would need to perform the duties they had been preparing for most of the previous year but never really expected to do in earnest. Men looked at each other with eyes that had been drowsy and half lidded moments before. White showed all around on most and everyone was quiet as they went about their preparations, even Johnny O'Donnell.

Jimmy was the last to make it into position, he had been long at the latrine. Sarge growled at him as he was dressing the line and went on. Ike heard his brother take a deep breath and looked his way in time to get a forced grin, a grin that he could now remember. "Well Ike, I think that elephant is about to arrive"

"Wish he'd waited until after breakfast." Ike replied. Both were trying to get their spirits up.

"Stand up there O'Donnell!" Sarge barked at Johnny. "Oh, you are standing up, I forgot." He said chuckling, trying to help relieve the tension by picking on Johnny.

"Half a league, half a league, half a league onward, all in the valley of death rode the six hundred." Jimmy quoted the Tennyson poem that he and Ike had memorized. As if to punctuate his sentence three booms from artillery could be heard to their south.

"Cannon to the right of them, cannon to the left of them, cannon in front of them, volleyed and thundered!" Ike said quickly before Jimmy could respond.

Johnny stood between the Lowery brothers, looking first at Jimmy and then at Ike as they recited their lines of poetry. For once he was speechless, the only poem he had memorized started out "There once was a lady named Cager," and somehow it didn't seem appropriate so he squared his shoulders and looked forward and tried not to shake.

"Forward March" came the call and the line moved forward. Ike remembered how it had been a relief to finally be moving, occupied with the mechanical action of motions practiced for months to the familiar sounds of bugles and drums. The regiment marched with as much precision as was possible as they dodged briars, shrubs, and saplings.

Shooting continued to their front as pickets and skirmishers from both sides exchanged fire. White tailed deer ran toward the regiment and leaped through the ranks of soldiers as if they weren't there. Rabbits and squirrels scampered about looking for cover and nearly tripped up a few of the marchers as they fled their homes in hopes of escaping the noise.

The blue line came to the edge of a weedy ravine and halted. On the far side of this small valley stood another line of men in blue uniforms. Both lines stood as if frozen and stared across at the other, there was no breeze and the flags hung limp. Most were convinced that these were enemy troops in spite of their colors. The cut of the uniforms was somehow different and their regimental flag didn't look right. The Colonel had spoken with his counterpart on the other side for a few moments when a small wind came up and floated the flag away from its pole. Someone pointed out that the flag was from Louisiana and the Colonel gave the order for his men to retreat by columns. The blue coats on the other side began to level their muskets in the direction of the Illinois men. The rim of the valley gave the Union men cover as they retreated with bullets whizzing and whining inches over their heads. They would learn some time later that this was a regiment from a Louisiana Military Academy, who were still in their blue Federal Uniforms for lack of any better.

"I think I know how them rabbits felt!" Johnny puffed as they were retracing their steps.

"I wish we could run as fast as those deer." Jimmy replied as they approached their campsite.

For the first time of many the regiment heard a sound that would chill their blood and resound in many nightmares for as long as they lived. The Confederates let loose the high pitched ululating scream that would be the last thing that many a Yankee soldier would hear in this world. Johnny would say later that the "Rebel Yell" sounded like Satan's rabbit dogs yelping after their prey.

The regiment marched past their camp and formed their next line on a slight elevation just beyond rifle range of the line of tents, where the enemy had stopped. The Colonel gave the order for them to lie down. There they waited for their pursuers. Their wait was extended as the Rebels looted the camp. They could see men running in and out of tents, pillaging for food and whatever spoils took their fancy. The commanding officer of the Louisiana Regiment berated his men and ordered them to stop their plundering and re-form. He had to fire his pistol in the air to get their attention and it took several minutes to get them back in to line. This activity gave the Illinois regiment time to prepare. They had the advantage of a row of sassafras saplings that had proliferated at the edge of the fallow field where they had stopped to face the enemy. Lying behind the raised root wads of the small trees gave them a small but effective cover.

Soon the enemy was coming towards them. The blue coated Louisiana men marched with the movements they had learned from Hardee's tactics, the same book the Illinois men had drilled from for months. When the Rebels came within range, the Colonel gave the order to fire. The blue line kept coming, but with frequent gaps where men had been felled. Ike had made one of those gaps, having killed the first of many secessionists he would fire upon in the months to come. The men scooted backwards and rolled on their backs to reload while others took their place on the firing line.

The Rebels stopped, took aim and fired at their attackers, but did little damage other than raining sassafras twigs on the heads of their foes.

Union artillery men were plying their trade and made even bigger holes in the approaching line. After two barrages of canister rounds the Confederates broke and began their retreat. With a loud 'hurrah' the Union Regiment rose and followed, stopping only to fire their guns at likely targets. As they gained on the Rebels, an occasional man would stop and take cover behind a tree and fire back. One of these managed to line up Jimmy in the iron sights of his musket. Ike's brother fell beside him. Ike dropped to the ground next to Jimmy and held him in his arms as he drew his last ragged breaths and coughed out his last words.

"Theirs not to...make reply, Theirs not to question why, Theirs but to....do and die......, Into the valley of death........." Jimmy said, his voice fading with the last words.

"Rode the six hundred." Ike said in response. Seeing that there was nothing else to do, he closed Jimmy's eyelids, picked up his gun and moved forward.

Johnny was standing over the man who had shot Jimmy, bayoneting his corpse again and again, crying and screaming curses at the bloody cadaver. Ike put a hand on the small man's arm as he thrust the bayonet once more into Jimmy's killer and stopped his butchery.

"I cain't give Jimmy back, but I killed that son of a bitch!" Johnny blubbered.

"I know Johnny, but we have to keep moving, we have to charge on, that's what we are here for!"

And charge they did, until Confederate artillery drove them back. They would spend the rest of the day charging and retreating, mostly retreating. Ike and Johnny stayed side by side through their first battle. By the day's end Ike felt as if in some way Johnny had become his brother.

Ike looked back up through the knothole at the stars, Orion had moved almost out of his limited field of vision while he had been reliving the day his brother died.

"Jimmy's up there with 'em now, Ikey." Johnny said. "He can still see the stars only better."

"You know that do you, Johnny?" Ike said, surprised by how grateful he was to hear his friend's voice again.

"Don't know a whole lot, but I know that." Johnny replied, sounding subdued and tentative.

"I hate to admit it, but I've missed you Johnny."

"Well, I've been here all along. I thought I'd give you a little peace and hush up for a while. I know I can be kinda' irritatin' sometimes. I even helped you write that letter, you seemed like you was havin' trouble."

"I remember when you couldn't read or write all that well." Ike said, remembering how he and Johnny had labored over an old primer. He had made some progress, but it had come slow until Johnny found a copy of "Fanny Hill" and his reading skills improved dramatically. Expressing his own thoughts on paper had still been a challenge, but he could recite the steamiest passages from his one book library by heart.

"Well, I wasn't so good when I was a livin' but I think I'm right good at it now. I might just have had a little help though."

One day while he was admiring a cloud formation through his small portal Johnny interrupted his thoughts. "You seem to be getting' purty comfortable down here, Ikey. The rest of the regiment is out there somewhere fightin' and you're here readin' all them books and lookin' at clouds."

"So you think I should try to escape again Johnny? Do you know something I don't know?"

"I always knew things you didn't know, Ikey!" He giggled. "I know even more now that I'm dead. I know you cain't break open

120

that door and run but you oughta' be keepin' an eye out for opportunities."

"Sometimes I think I'm too comfortable here, this cellar seems like a cocoon that protects me from the outside world. A part of me would be happy just to stay here where I'm safe and comfortable."

"I don't know it it's a cocoon or a womb Ikey. That ol' girl is tryin' to keep you all warm and snug here like it's gonna' protect you and her boy both. It may be comfortable Ike, but I ain't to sure that it's all that safe, it could turn into a tomb."

Ike tested the door again and found it to be immovable. The bar was always secured when Marcus left for any period of time. The weight, which Ike had seen when he and Marcus were removing the bodies of the two intruders, was an old grindstone that was rolled on top of the door as an added measure. Something about the round stone reminded Ike of Christ's tomb in an old Bible illustration. "Johnny, I wish someone would roll away the stone for me."

"Well, that's way above my rank, I'm afraid. I don't think I'm even a corporal yet."

"The only way I see to get out of here is to somehow rush out while Marcus has the door open, but he never leaves it unsecured except when he is coming and going. I don't think I would have a chance of getting past him, he's just too big." The thought of trying to fight his way past Marcus was daunting and the idea of doing something to harm him troubled Ike as well. In spite of his situation he was fond of the taciturn giant.

"Let's just keep a watchin' Ikey. Somethin' might just happen that you'd miss."

No lapses on the part of his guardian seemed to present any opportunities for Ike to flee. He resumed his reading of Sir Walter Scott's "Ivanhoe". The leather bound volume was well worn and Ike assumed it must have been a favorite of Dr. Pendleton and his sons. Inked on the fly leaf in an elegant hand was the inscription, "To Todd from his Father, Christmas 1859".

Late one afternoon as he was reading "Rob Roy" Ike heard hoof beats in the yard and quick booted steps in the house above. After the visitor left he could hear Mrs. Pendleton pacing back and forth in the kitchen above his abode.

"I think she got some bad news Ikey." Johnny said

"You don't suppose Todd is dead?"

"I don't think so, but she's pacin' back and forth like she's got a lot on her mind. Kinda' like you do sometimes."

A storm came that evening. Lightning flashes sent flickers through the knothole and the crack in the door. Something about the lightning disturbed Ike. Some old memory was trying to restore its place in Ike's conscious mind, but could not make its way through. "You scared o' lightin' there Ikey?" Johnny asked.

"No more than anyone else I suppose." Ike said out loud, not thinking to keep his conversation internal. He caught himself and looked around to make sure no living soul had heard him. Something about the lightning had unnerved him. "I think I had a bad experience with lightning once Johnny, but I cannot recall what it was. I just know that it was something terrible." He sat in silence watching the flickering and listening to the thunder.

"It's the noise of the thunder that always used to bother me Ikey. First time I heard artillery, I thought it was thunder, after that plain old thunder never seemed so bad." Johnny mused.

Whatever recollection wanted to be triggered by the storm, nothing came to Ike as he sat uncomfortably watching and listening. After a while the storm began to seem more like a portent of coming doom than a memory.

Some rain trickled down the steps, but for the most part the cellar remained dry, Ike watched as a small puddle formed under the knothole. Marcus brought his dinner at the usual time but was not accompanied by his mistress. Ike noted that the big man was wearing what looked like a Union Army poncho draped over his head as he carried the oilcloth covered tray. Ike wondered if this was the poncho that had been in his pack or if it was from one of his dead comrades. As was his custom, Marcus retreated back up the steps, closed the door and barred it. Ike ate in silence, he was not at all disappointed not to have Mrs. Pendleton's usual company at supper.

Marcus returned some time later to take away the tray and dishes. He hung the dripping poncho on the spike that had been driven into a mortared joint to hang Ike's mirror. As he prepared the tray for its trip back up the stairs a series of violent flashes of lightning illuminated another smaller figure descending the steps. Each flash revealed the silhouette in a different position. When the figure descended the last step and stood dripping on the stone floor the lantern light revealed Micheline Pendleton. She stood there breathing heavily.

"Missy, you shoudn'a come out in this weather. You catch you def a somethin." Marcus said, looking at the woman with concern and a trace of what Ike thought was fear.

"I had to check on our guest, Marcus. I am much concerned about his health." She said, ignoring the big man's concern. She was drenched to the skin, having come out with no umbrella or other covering to ward off the rain. Her hair was plastered to her skull and her clothing was soaked and clung to her body. For once she looked her age and then some. Ike found himself sharing Marcus' concern for the woman's health.

Mrs. Pendleton picked up the lantern and held it high so she could examine Ike. She scanned him from head to foot as he stood before her. She paid particular attention to his face and spent some time examining it. Her manner made him squirm as she stared into his eyes.

"Are you feeling well, young man?"

"Yes, ma'am, I'm fine. I think you should get dried off as soon as possible though, you're shaking. Please let Marcus take you upstairs and get you situated, he is concerned about you. I'll be fine."

Still staring at Ike as if he might be a vision she spoke slowly and flatly. "I received a troubling letter from General Forrest's staff today. Todd has been wounded, he will survive, but I'm afraid he will be marred for the rest of his life. I do not understand how this could have happened. I was so sure that he would be under God's care and would be spared from harm." She paused and began to sob. "It...isn't....fair. It...just....wasn't....supposed....to.....happen...this....way!" She said, her sobs punctuating the words as she spat them out. She collapsed into Marcus' arms and continued her crying.

Marcus carried his now wailing mistress back up the steps. The door was left open and Ike closed it himself to keep out the rain. He stood at the bottom of the steps and looked at the unbarred door.

"Ikey......this might be your chance." Johnny said softly as if someone else might be listening.

Ike listened to the footsteps above for a few moments. He looked around for anything that might be of use to him. He grabbed the poncho off the spike and took the knife from the serving tray and stuck it in the top of his right boot. He looked around the room that had been his home for months. His eyes fell on the Volume of Sir Walter Scott and he paused for a few moments as if thinking of bringing it with him.

"Ikey, you need to move...now!" Johnny's voice came with more urgency.

Ike swallowed hard and bolted up the steps. He took the steps two at a time, being careful not to make too much noise and started out into the rain. He stood in the yard and tried to decide on a direction.

"Go to your right Ike....now!" Johnny shouted. "The creek will be up so you got to go to higher ground....get movin' before you lose your nerve! Go around towards the road!"

Ike went around the side of the house and headed toward the lane that he remembered marching down in what seemed like some other life. He was stopped in his tracks however by the sight of the four graves. Carved wooden markers had been placed at the heads of each of the mounds. Grass and ivy had begun to cover them and flowers had been planted near the markers. He had the urge to stop and pray over the remains of his friends but Johnny was screaming at him to move on. A lightning flash revealed the name on one of the markers.... "Joseph Pendleton 1843 -1862"

"Ikey, you can't stop! You don't have time for that! Get into those woods, Marcus is comin' for you!"

Ike had just started toward the woods where the attackers had waited in ambush for his squad when something thumped against the back of his head and dropped him to the muddy ground. He was knocked unconscious before he could complete his escape.

Chapter 4 – Deuteronomy

Once again Ike awoke in darkness. His head throbbed and he felt feverish. A bandage was wrapped snugly around the top of his head and another looped downward over his right eye. He had to cough and when he did everything hurt even worse, especially his eye. He had never felt so miserable as he did at this moment. His chest was congested, his head hurt, and his eye, something was very wrong with his eye.

"Ikey, can you hear me?" Johnny's voice came sounding tentative.

"Yes, Johnny, I hear you. Where am I?"

"Back home in your cellar I'm afraid."

"What happened?"

"You didn't move fast enough. Marcus heard you come up the steps and he caught you and conked you in the head with a piece of stove wood so you wouldn't get away. He was mighty afraid that he killed you. The big fella carried you back down to the cellar like you was a baby or somethin'. He cried like a baby himself 'til he figured out your skull wasn't crushed. I think you may 'of got you a case of newmonie from bein' out in that rain."

"My eye, Johnny! What happened to my eye?" Ike moaned.

"She took it out, Ike. She kept a mutterin' about how her boy Todd lost an eye in a battle and it made her so plum mad at God for lettin' her boy get hurt that she decided to get even with him and take it out on you. I know it don't make no sense but that poor woman has just clean lost her mind."

Ike's aching head reeled with the realization of what had happened to him. The thought of having lost an eye was sickening. He felt like he was going to retch and went into another coughing fit and nearly passed out.

"Johnny, did Marcus help her?"

"No, he had went upstairs to get you some clean sheets and stuff and she came down here with an ole' black bag that musta' been her husband's. She did it quick while you was unconscious. She pulled it out and cut whatever holds it in with a scalpel and plopped it in a jar fulla' alkyhol or somethin' like she was a keepin' it to look at or give to her boy. She packed yer' eye hole with some cotton and salve to keep it from bleedin' and just wrapped you up like she was a settin' a broke leg or somethin'"

"Marcus come in and stood there like somebody pole axed him. She just looked at him and proceeded to wrap you up. He looked at her and looked at yer' eye in the jar and then he looked back at her kinda angry like. I thought for a minute he was a gonna' kill her or somethin'. He raised that big hand up like he was about to strike her down, then he stopped and just looked at his hand as he brought it down. He just stood there and stared at her like she was somethin' he'd never seen before."

"She finished with you and then she turned to Marcus just like what she was a doin' was the most normal thing in the world. She quoted a Bible verse to him; she said 'And if any mischief follow, then thou shalt give life for life, Eye for eye, tooth for tooth, hand for hand, foot for foot, Burning for burning, wound for wound, stripe for stripe.' And she started puttin' stuff back in that bag."

"Then ol' Marcus come back and says 'Thou shalt not avenge, nor bear any grudge against the children of thy people, but thou shalt love thy neighbour as thyself.'" Johnny said in a deep serious tone as if he was mimicking the way Marcus had spoken. "That woman stopped what she was a doin' like she had been slapped and then she just locked eyes with him. It was like they was makin' a contest out of it. Them two just stood there and stared at each other for a while until she finally blinked and started back up the stairs. The big fella' stayed a gazin' down at you and a lookin' sad. He dropped to his knees and closed his eyes and prayed. Now I 'seen lotsa' folks pray before but I never saw anybody look any more sincere about it than he did. He looked like one of them pictures of Jesus prayin' in the garden, I half expected him to sweat blood. They's a lot more to that big darky than most folks black or white. The way he rattled off that Bible verse I bet he can read 'bout as good as you can."

Ike lay and listened to Johnny's account. Any doubt about the reality of his personal ghost or guardian was forgotten for now, he was sure that things must have happened just as they had been described. "Johnny, do you think I'm safe?"

"You are for now, Ikey. I don't think Marcus will let her hurt you any more if he can stop her, but she's crazy as a bedbug and sneaky to boot. We need to get you out of here as soon as you heal up some. I sure wish I coulda' done somethin' to stop her from cuttin' on you like that Ike. I hollered and carried on all the while she was workin' on you. She even stopped and looked around once, but I didn't get through to her. I guess it's just not somethin' I'm allowed to do." Johnny paused for a few moments. "S'pose it coulda' been worse, Todd coulda' got his balls shot off like I did."

"Thanks for the cheerful thought." Ike responded. "I think I need to sleep now, Johnny."

Ike's dreams were populated with specters of hideously wounded men. There were men with arms and legs missing, men with massive disfiguring head wounds, men who had been burned so badly that their own mothers wouldn't recognize them and would be traumatized by the sight of them. He dreamed of walking up the path to his own home and seeing Emma. She turned her head to him and revealed a patch over her own right eye and then she screamed at the sight of him. Freddy was missing an eye as well and barked at Ike as if he were a stranger.

Nathan Bedford Forrest galloped through the landscape of Ike's subconscious. Ike had glimpsed Forrest briefly at "Fallen Timbers" and would long remember the man's striking appearance. Riding at the tall Cavalier's right hand was a one eyed young cavalryman. The rider had Ike's face and bearing and wore a black patch over his right eye. The blue left eye winked at Ike mischievously. He was dressed not in the uniform of the Confederacy but wore a plumed hat, tall boots, and the archaic regalia of a French Musketeer from an illustration in one of Jasper Pendleton's volumes. The rider looked at Ike and shouted cheerfully "Don't worry Ike; I still have another eye left!"

Forrest looked at Ike as well and chimed in "Yes, he still has an eye, and so do you.....for now!" before tilting his head back and laughing so loudly that it made Ike's head throb. The riders screamed "the Rebel Yell" and plunged into a cringing group of Yankees. Ike's own squad quaked as they were savaged by Forrest and his men. The laughing screeching Rebels slashed the blue coats with their sabers and trampled their victims under the hooves of their horses. Todd drew a massive wheel lock pistol and fired point blank at Sarge, whose head exploded in gore as the ball passed through his right eye.

Ike drifted in and out of consciousness for several days as his body fought to survive the ravages of his respiratory infection and the shock from the blow to his head and the loss of his right eye. Fever and chills alternated as he fought off infections for which there were no remedies available. More than once he stood at the brink of death and on one occasion he saw the dead members of his squad standing before him with welcoming smiles, his brother Jim was with them, looking as fit and proud as had been on the day he first received his blue uniform. There was a shallow stream between himself and his friends and his only thought was to cross it and join them. Johnny stepped forward and smiled "Not yet, Ikey! You got a thing or two left to do on that side old buddy!" Ike moaned in his sleep when he saw someone else among the small crowd awaiting him, someone else who shouldn't have been there.

In near lucid moments Ike saw Marcus staring down at him. The broad brown face showed anguish as the big gentle hands tended to Ike's needs.

Micheline Pendleton's face swam into his field of view on a few occasions. Her concern for his well being was obvious but she was kept at a distance. Ike sensed Marcus was keeping her from approaching too closely. She also appeared in dreams. One time she was carrying Ike's eye in a jar of clear liquid. The eye seemed to stare at Ike as the woman chanted "If thy right eye offend thee, pluck it out!"

After nearly two weeks of fighting for his life Ike's fever broke, his body had won out over the infection and he was beginning to heal. He was still weak from the ordeal but he was recovering. He was no longer coughing as much and he was awake more and able to think rather than merely dream.

When he was able to sit up and look around he noticed to his horror that there was a shackle on his left foot attached to a chain whose other end was fixed to a ring that had been mortared into the stone wall of the cellar. The shackle was padded with soft cloth apparently to keep it from chafing his ankle. The two halves of the shackle were held together on one side with a rivet and the other with a sturdy padlock that connected the whole affair to the end of the chain. It was obvious that Marcus sympathies went only so far. Ike was not meant to leave.

Ike stared at the old fashioned "smokehouse" style lock that kept him fettered. The keyhole stared back at him with a one eyed wink, as if it knew some secret knowledge that he had yet to discover.

Johnny murmured reassurances to Ike from time to time in what Ike thought might be his more sane interludes. The fact that he felt more rational having conversations with a dead man was disturbing in itself, but Johnny's voice was a comfort to him in his isolation. He couldn't escape the thought that somehow his mind had been affected by his original head wound during the ambush and Johnny was a symptom of the damage.

Ike had seen plenty of other soldiers who were mentally or emotionally impaired by either physical wounds or by the exposure to so much violence. Some merely sat and stared into space, seemingly unaware of their surroundings. Others developed tics and talked to themselves or spoke with invisible companions. The distinguishing difference between these men and their conversations and his communication with Johnny was that they talked out loud and ignored actual persons who were present. It was not unusual at all for soldiers to have night terrors and wake up screaming from having relived some battlefield horror beyond their conscious mind's ability to process during waking hours.

"Ikey, you must be gettin' a wee bit better. You're a layin' there with your eye open and thinkin' 'bout whether or not I'm real or some sort of mental problem." Johnny cackled.

"I don't know if you are a mental problem, Johnny, but I do believe that you had a mental problem when you were alive and you don't seem to have improved much."

"Why Ikey, I'm just as sane as you are!" Johnny said laughing raucously. "I know you're better now, since you're so cranky."

"Johnny, do you remember me standing beside a creek and seeing a crowd on the other side?"

"I was in that crowd Ikey. You were almost to the point of comin' over to us, but your time ain't at hand yet."

"Johnny, why did I see Emma with them?"

Johnny took a few moments to respond. Ike had the impression that his companion was consulting with someone else. "She's on the other side alright Ike. She's waitin' for you. I know you tried to forget that she died 'cause it was too painful for you to remember. You're gettin' stronger now and you're gonna have to deal with it sometime. Ikey, she says it wasn't your fault even though you somehow got it in your head that it was. The lightnin' hit the house and set it on fire. She tried to get out but she knocked over a lamp and the oil caught fire and it was over for her pretty quick. She said her last thoughts were about you."

"You talked to her?" Ike said, feeling a pang of something like jealousy.

"She loves you Ike. She always loved you, even when you was a drinkin' too much. She wants you to know that."

"Why can't I talk to her, why am I stuck with you?"

"Don't know Ikey, that's way above me. I don't think most folks even get somebody like me, you just seemed to need somebody and I had some work to do yet and here I am. Hey, you coulda' got ol' Charlie Olson and you know what a stutterer he was, and besides he didn't know you as well as I do."

"I need to get out of here more than ever Johnny, but now I'm chained."

"I think ol' Marcus might a lot more sympathetic now, he either has the key or knows where it is."

"But he's the one that put the chain on me I'm sure."

"And he might just be the one to unlock it too Ikey. Don't give up hope, it's one of them three important things the apostle talked about you know; faith, hope, and charity."

"You're starting to sound more like an angel."

"Well, I always liked it when people put things simple. Them three things always made sense to me, I cain't quote chapter an' verse like you and Mama Pendleton, I just know that it was Paul a writin' one of his letters, but I always tried to understand things on my level. Right now you need all three of those good things, I know that the last one may be pretty hard for you. It's gonna' be hard to be charitable towards that crazy woman, but I think you have to try to love your enemies. You got love on your side though, God loves you, Emma loves you, and I love you. I think that's one reason I got so lucky, you was the best friend I ever had and somehow that gave me the job of lookin' out for you to help redeem my sorry self."

"Thanks Johnny, you were always a good friend to me both in life and in death. You're right about something else, I am not in a loving mood toward Mrs. Micheline Pendleton right now. I saved her life Johnny, and she repaid me by taking out my eye and chaining me to a wall! The best I can do is not to pray for her to drop dead or burst into flames. I suppose I should have faith and pray for her mind to heal, that would be asking for a miracle. I should have just left her in the cellar and ran when I had the chance." He thought for a few moments and grew even angrier. "I should have set fire to this damned house with her in it and made my escape. The fire would have been a diversion to keep the Home Guard occupied."

"You couldn't have done that Ikey, you just don't have it in you to let someone die like that."

"I let Emma die!" Ike moaned out loud. "I should just have went into the flames with her, at least she wouldn't have died alone!"

"Johnny, I would have been better off if that confederate had done a better job of it and killed me that first day, I would be with Emma now instead of being chained up in this cellar with an eye missing and just waiting for a crazy woman to finish me off."

Ike slept again and dreamed of the time of Emma's loss. The flames came again and Ike knew what they meant. He had been drinking at a tavern and staggered toward home just in time to see the house engulfed in flames. He had run toward the structure and was trying to get in when his neighbors caught him and pulled him back. The burns on his hands and arms were excruciating, but the suffering from the loss of his wife was more than his mind could deal with. Enlisting in the army was a way to escape the life that was so full of reminders of Emma.

Mrs. Pendleton tried to converse with Ike on several occasions as he was recuperating, but Ike would only roll over on his side and face the wall. "You are angry with me Mr. Lowery and I suppose you have a right to be. The news I get from Todd reveals that he is recovering at about the same pace as you. I believe that I have gained God's attention for now and you both will survive this war and return to your homes and those who love you." When Ike remained silent she retreated up the steps. Before the door was closed she spoke loudly "...it is profitable for thee that one of thy members should perish, and not that thy whole body should be cast into hell."

"Matthew 5:29!" was Ike's only reply.

"That was quick, Ikey!" Johnny said in awe.

"It's a verse that has been on my mind lately.... and on hers too. It starts out with "If they right eye offend thee, pluck it out....'"

"That one always made me uncomfortable." Johnny sniggered. "I always wondered if I oughta' be cuttin' off somethin' that got me into trouble. That Johnny Reb took care of that for me."

Under Marcus care Ike recovered and grew stronger. He resumed his exercise and walking back and forth in the cellar. The chain had been carefully measured to allow him enough freedom to walk from one corner of the cellar to the other. He could make it up the steps far enough to gaze out of the knothole.

One day as he was pacing, Marcus brought him a small gift from his mistress. "This from Missy, she made it herself, she made one for Todd and one for you." Marcus said handing Ike the small package. It was a black silk eye patch. Ike sighed and looked at it for a long time, thinking of refusing it. "It'd mean a lot to her if you'd wear it. She wasn't in her right mind when she done it and she sorry for it now. This the closest she can do to givin' it back."

"She just wants to hide what she did to me. I saved her life and this is how she repaid me. Why should I help her cover up her guilt?" Ike spat out the last line with more anger than he had meant to convey.

"Marcus, she hasn't been in her right mind since I've been here. Sometimes she's better than others but not much. You know if Todd dies she will kill me."

"I won't let her do that. If I had know what she was gonna' do, I would 'a stopped her." Marcus said and then paused. "If I'd known she was this bad off I might have just let you go before this all happened. Trouble is, if you had escaped the Rebel army would probably have caught you anyway, and you might have lead them back to Missy and caused her trouble. If you had made it to your own army they might have caused her trouble too when they found out what she did to you. That situation is even worse now. I don't see any harm in you staying here. For now, I'm keeping you here for your sake and for hers, and maybe for my own."

"Hey, Ikey, Marcus is talkin' different!" Johnny observed, noting how contractions and mannerisms had left the man's speech like a snake shedding its skin.

"I noticed it too, Johnny." Ike thought. "He puts on the slave talk."

"Marcus. Why are you so devoted to her?"Ike asked.

The big man paused and looked at Ike for a long moment and then sighed. "I suppose I owe you an explanation. She is my sister, the only family I have."

"Your Sister?" Ike and Johnny said simultaneously as Marcus paused as if to gather his thoughts and consider what he was about to say.

"Her Father's....our Father's first wife died shortly after they were married. Our father, Julius Broussard, was somewhat of a loner, but he was lonely after his wife died. My Mother moved into the big house to look after things and the Master became infatuated with her, she was a very attractive woman, a good and intelligent woman. He treated her well and she fell in love with him. He sired me and treated me like the son I was. We kept to ourselves mostly, his plantation was off by itself and he wasn't one for social gatherings anyway. His family was furious that he was living with my Mother and me as if we were the family that we had truly become, but he paid them no mind. He was not one who felt he needed to be involved in society in order to be successful. He managed his affairs well and

144

had carved out a prosperous operation which he believed allowed him the freedom to live as he pleased. We were happy until my Mother became ill when I was about five. She was expecting again, and they were praying for a little girl. My Father sat by her bed with me and cried his eyes out when she died. He had her buried right next to his first wife in the family cemetery in spite of his siblings' protests."

Ike pictured a man mourning the loss of a wife and then another. The thought was poignant to him now that he was in the process of coming to grips with having lost Emma. As bad as it was having lost one wife, something in him wondered if losing a second would be any easier or would it be worse. He shook off the thought and re-focused his thoughts on Marcus' narrative.

"His sisters fixed him up with a white woman not long after. He was reluctant at first to meet her, said he wasn't ready yet but my aunts, who could barely stand to be in my presence insisted. The woman was a beauty, even more beautiful than Missy, and my Father, our Father, fell hard for her, and she for him. They were married soon after they met and she moved in and took over. She was nice enough to me when no one else was around, but I was to be a servant when there was company, and she involved herself more in the community and craved company far more than my Father did. I may be foolish to believe it, but I think she did it to protect me as much as to keep up appearances. She had Missy when I was seven. I thought that baby was the most beautiful creature I had ever seen. I looked after her and played with her and pulled her around in a little wagon. I was so proud of my little sister that I felt like I would explode, but I couldn't tell anyone.

By the time I was thirteen I was bigger than most grown men. People told my Father that I should be a field hand but he wouldn't hear of it. He wanted to keep me up at the house to look after Missy. He knew she'd always be safe when I was around and he knew that making me her personal servant would keep me out of the fields.

Missy grew up and was educated by her mother and a private tutor. I believe that even as a child she was different. She often seemed to live in an imaginary world. She spoke out loud to people who weren't there and insisted that I talk to them as well. She had long conversations with God, the prophets, the apostles, or whoever might have been in her daily Bible readings. Once she became convinced that I was Moses and I disappointed her by not being able to create her a dry path across the creek. Her parents and I worried at her actions but she was a happy and loving child and there seemed to be nothing any of us could do.

Missy liked to play school and she taught me everything she knew. I wasn't supposed to learn to read of course but our Father didn't care as long as I didn't let my knowledge show. He was proud of my progress. I read the books in his library and have read the Bible through a dozen times at least. Missy's mother was frightened by the fact that Missy had broken the rules by teaching me so much. She wanted my Father to send me away but Missy cried until she became ill and our Father wouldn't hear of it. My candle was kept under a bushel so to speak.

As she grew older, Missy seemed to understand that her behavior was disturbing to the rest of us and I believe she managed to control it or at least hide it most of the time. I sensed sometimes when she would have a spell and I would watch her closely. By the time she was in her early teens her voices seem to have left her. She confided in me once that she missed them and wondered if she had been abandoned.

When Missy was about fifteen her Mother became ill. She was confined to her room for weeks and the local Doctor could do little for her. Father was desperate and asked around and sent for someone more skilled at his craft. That's when we met Doctor Jasper Pendleton. He examined Missy's Mother for a long time and went outside with Father to talk. Doctor Pendleton told Father that his wife was a going to die but it might take a long time. He could give her medicine for the pain so she would be comfortable, but that was about all anyone could do. Our Father didn't want to accept the hard truth. He and Jasper went for a walk to discuss Missy's mother's condition. Something in the young man's manner convinced him that he was going to lose yet another wife. They were coming back into the house when Jasper Pendleton saw Missy for the first time. The young Doctor lost his heart the moment he laid eyes on my little Sister. He was a gentleman and very respectable about it but he set his mind on her right then and there. He kept coming back to see about Missy's Mother and did all that was possible to alleviate her pain, but she was gone inside of six months. By that time Missy had fallen in love with the Doctor and our Father saw that it was a good thing and gave his blessing to their marriage.

By the time of Missy's marriage the plantation was in trouble, Father had let things go while he looked after his wife as she was dying and he was too overwrought after she died to pay attention to it. He had entrusted the operation to a bad overseer who lost through mismanagement what he didn't outright steal. I was sent along as part of Missy's dowry when she and Jasper got married so I couldn't be sold off.

My Father had tears in his eyes as we parted. Jasper had inherited this farm which was many miles away and we would not be able to visit often due to the distance. My Father looked at me and told me how proud he was of me as a son. His last words to me were to ask me to please look after Missy. It was an easy promise to make; I would have walked through fire for her anyway, I still would."

Ike winced at Marcus' mention of walking through fire. The opportunity to walk through fire for someone meant more than a figure of speech to him. He looked down at the old scars on his hands as the other man continued his story.

"That was the last time we saw our Father. He was standing on the porch of the big house as we drove away in Jasper's carriage. Later that week he lay down in the cemetery where the three women he had loved were buried and shot himself, he was so far in debt that there was little inheritance for Missy except for me. She had only Dr. Jasper and me to look after her.

So I made my life with Missy and Jasper. Jasper treated me well in the beginning, he knew I was Missy's half brother and I believe he thought of me as family. He was a very good and successful Doctor and made enough money to support his family well. I oversaw the place and looked after the crops and livestock and the other slaves who worked for us. I also helped them raise their boys. You never saw five more lively boys than that bunch." Marcus finished, shaking his head and remembering. "I was always 'Uncle Marcus' to them, even when they left for the war."

Marcus looked grave and paused for a while as he seemed to gather his thoughts and dredge through old memories. Ike sensed that this was the first time the man has spoken of these things to anyone.

"Things were as nearly idyllic as most could have asked for in our lives here. Missy had her husband and her sons. I had work to do and people to care for. I was even married for a time, but like my Father before me, my luck was bad and my wife died giving birth to our son. The child only lived a few days." Marcus paused again as he recalled his personal tragedies. Ike felt a wave of sympathy for a man who had suffered a similar loss to his own. He wanted to tell Marcus about Emma, but held back as the big man resumed his narrative.

"Then the dark times started, Dr. Jasper wasn't a bad man at first but he had more ambitions than he wanted to admit. He mortgaged his farm to buy more land and more slaves to work it. He developed a taste for finer things, brandy, cigars, and fast horses for the boys. He was in the process of building a mansion for Missy on the next hill over when the war started. She insisted she was happy with the house they had but Jasper aspired to live the life of a gentleman planter and give her the type of home that she had grown up in. His idea of what a home was had become so much about keeping up with or outdoing the other 'aristocrats' that he ceased to be the man that Missy had fallen in love with. She still loved him, but he had pulled away from her, being more concerned about appearances and social status.

I refused to beat the slaves and work them like animals so he hired a white overseer named MacGregor and relegated me to being a house servant again. The new overseer had come from deeper in the South and was unmerciful to the field hands and their families. He convinced Jasper that his ways were best. The children were looked at as a saleable resource and breeding more for sale became a source of income.

I was angry at the treatment of the slaves. I had known many of them for years and thought of them as family. I had treated them well and they produced crops with as much efficiency without the cruelty that MacGregor insisted on, but Jasper would not see the folly of turning his operation over to this beast of a man. Jasper had began to see things in a different light himself.

As the boys grew they came to look upon the slaves as livestock, whose sole purpose was to make money to sustain the life they sought. They still treated me with respect in their mother's presence but I felt them pull away from me as they grew older. MacGregor winked at them when they trifled with the young slave girls. He was elated when the girls got pregnant and bore lighter skinned children that could be sold off as house servants. Jasper had sunk to the point of selling his own grandchildren. He thought he had kept Missy from knowing what was going on, but I think she knew even though she wouldn't acknowledge it.

The overseer resented my status in the family. He insinuated that a man of my size should be doing more to produce income.

Missy was called away to visit a cousin who had fallen ill and the man saw the opportunity to work his wiles. MacGregor knew he would never be allowed to turn me into a field hand but saw in me an opportunity for breeding stock.

MacGregor tried to befriend and beguile me to "get friendly" with the slave women in hopes of producing "bucks" of my stature. He coerced me to walk down to the quarters with him one evening, thinking he could get me drunk and put me out to stud. I resisted and he had two other men jump me and chain me up in an old log smokehouse, they poured liquor down me until I was in a fog. That chain on your ankle was once on mine."

Marcus paused again and gazed out the door as he recalled his confinement. Johnny couldn't help but comment. "Time was, I woulda wanted that job Ikey."

"I'm sure the overseer would have loved to have a bunch of short red headed bucks, who burned and blistered in the sun." Ike replied silently.

Marcus turned back to Ike and resumed his narrative.

"One by one, women were brought to me, stripped naked and pushed through the door. The first of these women wasn't terribly attractive but she seemed amused by the situation and acted as if she were willing and eager. She taunted me and aroused my lust and provoked me to do as I had been bidden. I was inside her and near the point of no return when she moaned in satisfaction and whispered in my ear. "You and me can jus' make Massa' another little nigger to go to the fields..." I stopped as if cold water had been thrown on me. She laughed at me as I lay panting and spilling my seed on the ground. She kissed my forehead and smiled. "Dey' said you was a good man, an' you is....jus' think about what I say nex' time." She pounded on the door and shouted at the overseer's lackey "Nigger done his bid'ness, let me outta here fo' he wear me out!"

The next woman was the widow of a man who I had been acquainted with for years. She was a beautiful and shapely being whose form I had always found enticing. I had resolved not to take advantage of the situation, but I have to admit to having a desire for her. She stood before me silently for a few moments as I looked at her with lust and chided myself for being tempted. As I was trying to think of something to say to her she did something I did not expect, she dropped to her knees in an attitude of prayer. Her action put out the flames of my lust and instead of taking her carnally I joined her in prayer. I put my shirt over her and held her in my arms and comforted her and we acted out a ruse that would be repeated several times. I did considerable moaning and she screamed as if in pain. The lackey grinned like a gargoyle as she staggered out melodramatically, crying with relief instead of the anguish of a raped woman.

I must have repeated my act with all the slave women the overseer thought capable of bearing a child. The women had communicated among themselves that I wasn't the beast I was intended to be and they seemed to try to outdo each other with their wailing and complaining. When they finally let me out MacGregor seemed pleased with himself and with me. A few weeks later he growled that I was even more useless than he thought.

When Missy returned things were back to normal, I had taken care of the house and garden and no mention was made of my other duties. I was as unhappy as I had ever been. Jasper and the boys had turned from being people I cared about as family to being shameful loathsome monsters. Had it not been for my attachment to Missy, I would have went North with long ago, but I could not leave her. She had loved Jasper deeply from the beginning and the change in him was a great loss to her. Seeing her sons degenerate was even worse. I could tell she was listening for her voices again.

When the war fever came Jasper stopped work on the big house and put his energies into helping equip a regiment so that his boys could go to war with the North as true Southern Gentlemen. I was glad to see them leave in spite of the pain it brought their mother. Within months four of them were dead, two died of camp fever early on and another two died at Shiloh charging into something that was referred to as the "hornet's nest". The loss of his sons took Jasper's health and finally his life. It seems to have taken Missy's mind.

Ike had seen the aftermath of the "hornet's nest". Bodies clad in gray and butternut were strewn about in great abundance where they had fallen in one failed charge after another as they attempted to take the position so tenaciously occupied by General Prentiss and his men. He wondered if he had stepped over or around one of the Pendleton boys as his regiment pressed the Confederates back on the second day of fighting.

A few days after Jasper died Missy and I went over the hill to the framework of the manor house. She sat on the beam that was to have supported the front porch and looked off into the distance for hours. I stayed with her for a while, but I decided that she needed to have some time to herself so I came back here to see to some chores. Just as the sun was beginning to set I saw smoke, Missy had brought matches with her and had set the big house ablaze. I had a team already hitched to a wagon I had just unloaded and I beat those poor animals unmercifully as I drove them over the hill. Missy stood facing the conflagration that was to have been Jasper's monument to himself. I was thankful that the wind was to her back or she might have been scorched by the fire. She didn't speak for days afterward. She finally willed herself to live for the hope that Todd might eventually return to her.

With Jasper and the boys gone MacGregor tried to romance Missy in hopes of gaining ownership of the plantation. She loathed him and spurned his advances. She threatened to fire him, but he threatened to go to the authorities and tell them that she had taught me to read if she did. She wasn't sure what the outcome might be, but she didn't want to find out either, so MacGregor stayed on, abusing the slaves and harassing Missy. He had an unfortunate accident one night shortly after their last argument and now resides at the bottom of that old well out by the barn." Marcus paused and looked at Ike to gauge his reaction. He smiled as he went on. "The local authorities spent little time looking for him and it was assumed that he had left for greener pastures, no one seemed to miss his presence and there was a war going on. His horse and worldly goods seemed to be missing as well. I believe his horse may have defected to the Union.

A few of the original slave families stayed on and have been sharecropping. We make enough to feed ourselves and maintain a fair standard of living for Missy. The later acquisitions slipped away and followed your army I believe. I hope they are able to make better lives for themselves. Were it not for Missy, I would be somewhere to the north by now. If your army would have me at my age I might even be carrying a rifle."

Ike had listened attentively to Marcus' story. He looked down at the chain on his ankle and thought of the irony of a white man being chained by a black one.

Marcus had been having the same thought. "It does seem backwards doesn't it? I have to admit to a perverse pleasure in chaining up a white person. Please don't take it personally, I bear you no ill will and I intend to free you as soon as I am convinced that doing so will bring no harm to Missy. I thought keeping you here in the first place was a bad idea, but she insisted on it and I did feel that you would be treated brutally by the home guard or the Confederate army. I hate to admit it but when I found you it was as if I was hearing one of Missy's voices in my head and I was concerned that I was losing my mind as well, but thankfully the annoying voice went away."

"Annoyin' voice! What's he mean by that, Ike?" Johnny chortled. "I wish I could annoy him into lettin' you go, but for some reason I can't penetrate his ol' black noggin any more, but it sure was fun when I did."

"You speak well, when you want to." Ike opined.

"It's a habit I have. When there are strangers around I use the slave vernacular. Among our family I speak normally, the way I learned to talk in my childhood. It seems that the sound of a black man speaking better English than most whites makes many southerners very uncomfortable, so I try to keep them at ease by speaking 'slave talk'. I suppose you have been here so long I am beginning to look on you as family and have lapsed into my normal manner of speaking."

"I think it's time for me to get your supper." The big man said with a grin. "Do you play Chess Mr. Lowery?"

"Yes, I do. And please call me Ike."

"Well ain't that a wonder!" Johnny said.

"Yes it is. I think you were right, Marcus seems to be at least sympathetic, even if he isn't inclined to let me go."

"He may be, but that woman is smart and sneaky, even if she is crazy. She could put one over on the both of you if you don't watch her."

Ike looked at the eye patch and looked at his sunken socket in the small mirror Marcus had placed on the wall for him and decided to try it on. "That there patch makes you look kinda' dangerous there Ikey. With the patch and the black beard you look like one of them pirates in the story books. Hope you don't end up with a wooden leg or a hook fer a hand."

"Hush Johnny, I don't want to think about that."

After supper, Ike and Marcus played chess. Marcus brought a well worn chessboard with finely carved pieces and sat it on the table after he had taken away Ike's tray.

"You want to be white, I suppose." Marcus said with the trace of a grin.

"Well, since you are in the service of the white queen anyway, I think it would be fitting if you took the white pieces." Ike said, training his left eye on Marcus to read his expression.

Marcus looked at Ike for a long moment, trying to judge if his comment were out of bitterness or playfulness. He shook his head and began arranging the white pieces, starting with the queen.

As Ike had guessed, he was outmatched by his opponent. Johnny grumbled in his head. "I always liked checkers.....never could keep track of who could do what in this one."

Mrs. Pendleton descended the stairs and watched the game for a while. She sat on the footstool and studied the two men's moves. Ike ignored her completely and Marcus barely acknowledged her. She looked approvingly at the patch over Ike's empty eye socket for a few minutes and took her leave when it became obvious that Marcus was going to win.

Chapter 5 – Exodus

One morning Ike thought he heard thunder when he awoke. Soon after gaining consciousness he realized the sound was an artillery battle. Knowing that the sound could carry for miles in some instances he strained his ears to try to determine where it might be coming from. His experience with the sound of artillery told him that the battle was a small one, the spacing of the shots was such that he suspected no more than a half dozen pieces were involved. He also knew that geography and weather conditions could make a distant battle sound as if it were nearby and an entire artillery battery could be firing over the next hill and be barely audible.

He was straining his ears to hear what was going on when Marcus came down with his breakfast. "The battle is way over by Oxford as best as I can tell. Seems a Yankee regiment has been pursuing some of Chalmer's cavalry and they are jousting for a while. If the Union men aren't careful they will be surrounded and cut off."

"How do you know so much about it Marcus?" Ike asked.

News travels fast here. We Africans communicate with jungle drums, don't you know!"

How far are they from us?" Ike asked.

A good five miles or better" Marcus responded, placing Ike's tray carefully as if nothing of importance was happening. The noise diminished within a few minutes and life returned to normal in the cellar.

The following evening, Marcus had more news of the engagement. "It seems that your comrades pursued General Chalmers' men to a point within view of a neighboring plantation. Your artillery men unlimbered in the front yard and began ranging in on the mounted troops as two young women watched them from the veranda. The cannoneers put on a fine show for the damsels. Not to be outdone the rebel cavalrymen dodged the solid shot by quickly sidestepping their horses and bowing as the balls sailed past them. Two of the young fools were blown out of their stirrups as your comrades switched over to canister rounds. The maidens were appalled at the actual sight of bloodshed and retreated into their home just as the Union commander came up and lambasted his men for using up so much powder and shot and pulled his regiment out before they could be flanked by Chalmers."

"Marcus, what else do you know about how the war is going?" Ike asked. "Do your jungle drums tell you if there is any end in sight?"

"I don't know how far away the end might be, but your army took Vicksburg back in July and on the same day out east there was an awful battle in Pennsylvania." He paused as if trying to remember something. "Gettysburg was the name of the town I believe, and again the Union forces won it, but at a terrible price. Unfortunately men like Jefferson Davis and Robert E. Lee don't give up easily. The South will likely lose, but they will fight on until they have lost everything they thought they were fighting for. Their arrogant pride won't let them lay down their arms easily."

"I should be fighting with my regiment, instead of waiting here for the war to end or for your mistress to kill me." Ike said, hoping not to anger Marcus but also hoping to goad him into releasing him.

"Sometimes I think I should be fighting too." Marcus said. "I know the Union has finally allowed my people to join your army and engage in combat. We have much more of a stake in this fight than you do, but I am likely too old and I have an obligation to my sister."

"If you let me go, I can go back to fighting and you can take care of your sister." Ike said, thinking he probably had nothing to lose by asking.

"I am sure you would go back and win the war single handedly, but I think your comrades are doing quite well without you.....or me." Marcus replied as he headed back up the steps.

The thought of his own army being so close made Ike restless. He paced back and forth in his small abode, praying for deliverance even if it would put him back in the firing line. Ike was so engrossed in thinking of returning to his comrades that he forgot and wrapped his chain around a chair and started dragging his furniture around the room. Johnny chortled at Ike's antics as he nearly tripped over the footstool as he tried to regain his dignity.

Micheline Pendleton was also restless. She had not heard from Todd in weeks. She seemed to have lost weight and looked pale to Ike on the few occasions when she ventured down to check on his well being. Ike was polite, if distant when they spoke. Marcus always barred the door and rolled the grindstone onto it when he left for any amount of time so that his Sister would not be able to enter the cellar without him.

Ike could see that the strain of not knowing about her son was taking a toll on the woman. He managed to feel sympathy for her in spite of his situation.

"Mrs. Pendleton, you do not look well. I think you should eat something." Ike said one evening while his captor was watching the nightly chess game.

"I am grateful for your concern young man, but I have no appetite. I feel that I have been forsaken by God. I will fast until I hear from my son, or until I die."

Marcus looked at the woman and sighed. "Missy, God doesn't make deals. His ways are not ours and we can't bend him to our will. I don't believe that you can make him budge by starving yourself...........or anything else." He said, looking sideways at Ike.

"She's a hurtin' for sure Ikey." Johnny said. "You gotta' pray fer those that persecute you, but try to get out of their way when you can."

"I don't know the chapter and verse on that one Johnny, but I think you're right."

Ike was troubled with dreams again that night. The flames that had consumed his home and his wife tormented him. Scenes from the war moved through his mind as if to review the violence he had seen and participated in. He saw his squad being riddled with bullets in the nearby yard once more and heard their screams as they died.

The last dream that he could remember upon waking found him standing on the bank of another creek like the one where he had seen his friends and Emma, but this didn't feel like the same stream, it seemed colder and wider than the one where those who had loved him in life had stood and offered their solace. This time the weather was cooler, only starlight and a quarter of a waning moon illuminated the lonely place where he stood. Somehow he knew that the water was black. The moon was briefly obscured by a cloud and Ike could barely see anything when a lone figure appeared in the distance riding toward the creek on a tall cavalry horse. The clopping of the iron shod hooves on the stony ground echoed in his head like hammer blows on an anvil. Ike thought of this creek as the river Styx, where the one he had seen before seemed to him to be the Jordan. The figure stood and seemed to be staring directly at him when the cloud drifted away and bathed the watcher in moonlight. The horse's coat shone white as the cold light illuminated it. The rider doffed his broad brimmed hat and held it across his chest as he tilted his head in Ike's direction. The rider stared at Ike with one blue eye. A familiar looking patch graced the spot where another had once been. The figure raised his chin, and returned the hat to his head. Just before the rider turned the horse Ike noticed a dark stain across the midsection of the man's uniform. Even in the moonlight, Ike knew it was blood.   The mounted man clopped slowly back away from the water's edge as the moon was once again hidden.

Ike woke early that morning with the certain knowledge that Todd Pendleton was dead.

Did you see him last night?" Johnny asked. His voice was solemn for once.

Yes I did, Johnny, he was riding a pale horse. My time here is getting short isn't it?"

Well, I always heard that death rides a pale horse, but I don't rightly know who that horseman is a comin' for..."

Johnny's musing was cut short by a shriek from the house above. Mrs. Pendleton wailed and shouted. "My God, My God, why hast thou forsaken me?"

"Sounds like she had the same dream Ike."

She will kill me now if she can." Ike said, looking down at his chain.

"Change is comin' Ike, I can't see what it's gonna' be, and I don't think it'll be too purty..." Johnny trailed off as if lost in thought. Ike wondered if his old friend was trying to spare him with his uncharacteristic silence.

Marcus was later than usual bringing breakfast. He was as withdrawn as he had been when Ike had first arrived. He looked down and wouldn't look Ike in the face to answer his unspoken question. He was placing Ike's breakfast tray on the table when he jumped at a sound behind him. The cellar had been bathed in morning sunlight until a slender shadow partially blocked the stairway.

Marcus stood in front of Ike, presenting him with a view of his expansive back. "Missy, please go back, this is wrong and you know it." He said. Ike's blood seemed to freeze in his veins as he stood behind the wall of the big man's body and tried to peer around it.

"Ikey, stay calm and be ready to move. She's comin' for you." Johnny said in what sounded like a stage whisper.

"I know Johnny, I know. I've been expecting this from the beginning. No matter what happens, I'm glad you're here with me, whether you're real or just my imagination.

Who knows, maybe I get to cross that creek today."

"Cain't see even a short way into the future, but I just don't think it's your time yet. Just keep yer' eyes.....yer' eye open."

Ike still couldn't see anything but the backside of Marcus as he stood fully erect and faced his Sister. There was silence for a few moments as the two faced off Ike heard the clock upstairs chime eight times and mentally calculated that he would not be here to hear it strike once for the half hour.

"Step away, Marcus, I don't want to hurt you." The woman's voice came from the foot of the stairs.

"Why do you want to do this Missy, you haven't heard from Todd yet." Marcus said. The big man's tone was that of an adult talking to a misbehaving child.

"Oh yes I have Marcus, Todd is dead and you know it. You intercepted the letter from General Forrest. You wanted to protect me......or him.....from the truth." The woman said.

"What makes you think that Missy. You don't know that." Marcus said. Ike thought he heard a trace of panic in the man's voice.

"You know it's true Marcus. Todd told me that 'Uncle Marcus' kept the letter."

"Missy, you're imagining things. You haven't eaten in days and you are sick. Let me take care of you. Things will look different when you've rested and something to eat. Please Missy."

"Todd came to me last night and told me all about it. He was shot off his horse by a Yankee private just like our Mr. Lowery here. He suffered terribly. He was shot in the stomach and lingered for hours in pain and now he's dead. My beautiful son's soul is wandering the earth looking for justice, I have to give it to him. My last son is dead Marcus. I have nothing to live for, except to even the score. I am going to see to it that Mr. Lowery suffers the same end as Todd. I probably should have just killed him quickly in the beginning to spare Todd the suffering, but you talked me out of it. Now step aside Marcus so I can finish this now!"

"No Missy, don't!" Marcus boomed. "Give that to me before you hurt someone!"

"Marcus Aurelius Broussard......move aside now!" The woman screamed, making Ike's ears ring even more than usual.

Marcus lunged forward in an attempt to disarm his sister. Ike saw his body shudder as what sounded like a clap of thunder reverberated throughout Ike's small abode. The too familiar smell of burnt gunpowder and blood filled the small space.

The shot made Ike's ears ring worse. In the close quarters of the cellar, the sound was like standing next to an artillery piece. Marcus' stumbled sideways and knocked over the table, scattering crockery and silverware all over the cellar. Micheline Pendleton stood looking down at the body of her half brother, who had loved her from the time she drew her first breath. She watched as he drew his last. She knelt and put her hand on his forehead and spoke softly. "Marcus, I am so sorry, I didn't want to do that. You were the last person on this earth that loved me. Now I am truly alone."

One tear slid out of the corner of her eye as she gazed at Marcus. She took a deep breath and turned toward Ike.

The sympathy that had been on the woman's face a second ago was gone. He pupils were fully dilated showing black pools that made Ike think of the water in the river where he had been saluted by Todd Pendleton.

Micheline Pendleton was holding a pistol, possibly the largest pistol Ike had ever seen. The French made LeMat was massive, Ike had heard of the LeMat, but had never seen one, and would like not to have seen this one. The gun had a nine round cylinder that rotated around a second barrel which was that of a 16 gauge shotgun. The black maw of the shotgun barrel was smoking, having discharged its load of buckshot into Marcus. Mrs. Pendleton manipulated a lever on the hammer so that the gun would fire again from one of its other chambers and pointed it at Ike's midsection. She held the gun in both hands.

"I don't think she's bluffin' this time Ike, don't know a lot about them French pistols, but after what she did to Marcus, I s'pect this one's loaded." Johnny rasped.

"I had hoped and prayed that it would not come to this Mr. Lowery, I believed that this was going to work out so well, but I was deceived by Satan. This has all been just a trick of his to lure me down to perdition. You seem to have been a pawn in his game, a white pawn...." She looked down at Marcus briefly and said. "I suppose Marcus was my black knight. I am going to shoot you, then I am going to set this house on fire, and then I am going to shoot myself. No one is left to claim this house except the bank and they will only find ashes. I may be going to Hell for this, but I will not go alone." She stood looking at him and cocked the hammer. The click of the mechanism sounded to Ike like the gates of that same establishment slamming shut.

"Ikey, the chain!" Johnny shouted. His voice seemed so loud to Ike that he flinched and as he did he looked down and saw that Micheline Pendleton had stepped over the chain that led from Ike's left foot to the ring in the wall. Just as her finger was tightening on the trigger Ike swung his leg violently, whipping the chain around and pulling the woman's feet out from under her.

The explosion was another thunderclap, made louder by the fact that there was not a large man between himself and the gun's muzzle this time. Ike had flung himself toward the floor as he tripped up his would be killer with the chain. The bullet missed him by mere inches, caromed off two of the stone walls, and buried itself in one of the floor joists above, sprinkling sawdust into the already clouded air. The combination of the chain pulling her feet out from under her and the recoil of the LeMat threw the woman back against the stone wall. The back of her skull was impaled on the nail that had been driven into the mortar joint to hold Ike's mirror. She hung there against the wall with her eyes open. She assumed her characteristic intense stare for a moment and then her eyes seemed to lose their focus as her limbs sagged and her jaw dropped open. Micheline Pendleton was dead.

Ike blinked and looked at the chaos that surrounded him. Gun smoke and rock dust swirled in the air. Larger particles flashed in the bright sun light that came down the stairway. His hearing seemed to be gone.

"Johnny, are you still there?" Ike said out loud, barely hearing his own spoken words.

"She missed me, Ikey, but I thought for sure the ricochet was gonna' get me." He said with a little chuckle and then interjected "Merciful God!"

"That sounds like swearing, Johnny."

"No, I'm talkin' about the real thing here Ike. I just saw the two of them floatin' out of here. She looked confused at first, then Marcus took her hand and they just looked up that stairway into the light. They both looked back at you and smiled to see that you were alright. I ain't never swearin', Ikey, I was just talkin' about a merciful God."

"I'm glad, Johnny, that's comforting to know." Ike said standing up and dusting himself off. He looked around the cellar and took stock of the situation and then moaned. "Johnny, I could use some of that mercy myself. I have a few problems here. I'm truly grateful not to be gut shot and dying with the house burning down around me, but I am chained to the wall of this cellar with two corpses and a wingless angel for company. Marcus never did say what he did with the key to this lock."

"Better search his pockets, Ikey."

Ike was loath to touch Marcus but he gingerly went through each item of clothing to check for the key. The thought of finding that key burned in Ike's imagination as he tried to not think too much about the alternative.

"Ikey, you don't s'pose Mama Pendleton had the key?" Johnny said tentatively.

Ike found it hard to even approach Mrs. Pendleton. Her eyes were still open and seemed to stare straight at him as he scanned her clothing for pockets. He noticed a delicate chain around her neck and out of curiosity he pulled it out of her shirtwaist and discovered a locket. The locket was still warm from contact with her skin as he studied it. It popped open to reveal two small pictures, one of a young Micheline and the other a young Marcus. Ike looked into the youthful faces and thought of the people they had been in a happier time. He jumped at the sound of the clock striking the half hour and dropped the still open locket and let it fall to the woman's breast. The pockets of her skirt contained nothing but a handkerchief.

Ike scanned the cellar as if there were answers that would reveal themselves to him. He righted one of the chairs and the table and picked up silverware and salvageable food items. Two biscuits were still warm and wrapped in a napkin. A fried egg and some bacon were scattered too close to the chamber pot for Ike's comfort, but he knew food might be a serious issue very soon. The water pitcher had been broken and none remained. Only the cup and a saucer remained intact. He arranged the food items on the table as if breakfast had not been interrupted by bloodshed and looked around once more. He nibbled on a biscuit until he realized how thirsty it made him. He closed his eyes and prayed.

The first thing he noticed when he opened his eyes was the pistol laying against the wall. He stared at it for a few minutes and thought of its possibilities. He thought of using it to shoot the lock off the shackle, but remembered how Mrs. Pendleton's shot had caromed around the cellar. Another darker thought entered his mind. If he was unable to free himself from the chain and thirst, starvation, and the stench of the two corpses became too much he could free himself in another way.

"That's a coward's way out, Ikey and you know it." Johnny said. "You can come up with somethin' better than that. You always was one of the smart fellas."

Ike explored his other options. The ring in the wall had been anchored too well for him to pull it out. He stuck the barrel of the pistol in the ring and tried to turn it in hopes of loosening it but it would not budge.

He studied the mechanism of the lock and tried to remember how its internal members functioned. He and his brother had taken an old lock apart once and he tried to remember the shape of the tumblers. He had a vague Idea that he could bend a time of his fork and use it as a pick. This idea did not work.

As daylight faded he realized that not only did he not have matches or even a lamp. He was tired and hungry and incredibly thirsty. He ate the rest of the biscuit he had started earlier and regretted it. "There's always the chamber pot Ikey." Johnny giggled. "You just have to strain out the chunks."

"Thanks Johnny, that's just brilliant." Ike responded internally. He took a small satisfaction from realizing that he had not spoken this response out loud.

With nothing else he could do in the darkness of the cellar Ike lay down on his bed and tried to sleep. Sometime in the early hours of the morning he woke and saw that the moon had risen and was casting a pale light down the stairway. He thought that it would give him enough illumination to see his way to the chamber pot and part with some of the last precious liquid his body retained.

As he started to get up he saw a dark shape lumbering down the steps. An opossum had picked up the scent of death and was eager to see what pickings were available. Ike picked up the pistol, sighted down the long barrel with his one eye, cocked the hammer, and squeezed the trigger. Instead of the expected violence of an explosion there was only a dull click. The hammer had been damaged when the gun hit the floor after its last performance and would not descend all the way to contact the igniter pin. Ike tried it again and again. The noise startled the opossum into stopping on the last step from the bottom. The creature froze in position, aware that there was something still alive amid the tantalizing odors of early decay that were guiding its sensitive snout to an anticipated feast.

The sight of the opossum had repulsed Ike. He cocked the pistol again, advancing the cylinder to another live round. Again the gun only clicked. In a fit of rage he drew back to throw the gun at the scavenger. "I don't think that's a good idea Ikey!" Johnny said as Ike flung the weapon towards the Opossum.

The pistol just missed the hissing scavenger on the step. The hammer hit the step with enough force to drop it onto the igniter pin of the cartridge and the resulting explosion sent the opossum scurrying back up the steps. The bullet shattered Ike's drinking cup and caromed off the back wall before it buried itself in Marcus gut. The puncture opened a hole in the dead man's intestine and released a hideous smell that made Ike gag and lose what little food was left in his stomach.

"I told you that was a bad one Ikey!" Johnny chirped.

"Shut up!" Ike said, realizing that he had spoken out loud this time.

Johnny maintained his silence for a while as Ike regained a little of his composure. The shaken man completed his trip to the chamber pot and lay back down to rest until dawn. He prayed for daylight and deliverance.

"You never did like the taste of 'possum much anyway, Ikey" Johnny said, giggling as Ike drifted back to sleep.

Ike woke to what he thought was the sound of cannon fire, but it was only thunder accompanied by blessed rain. He stood in the stairwell and felt the refreshing drops. He opened his mouth and caught enough water to moisten his parched throat and realized he had nothing to catch water in. He went as far up the steps as his chain would allow him but he could only get his head above the rim of the opening to see a little of the muddy back yard.

Descending the steps he looked around and saw only one vessel that could possibly hold water. He grabbed the chamber pot and carried it up the steps to his limit and hurled its contents as far as he could out into the yard. By now the drizzle had turned into a steady rain that yielded him enough water to rinse the worst of the smell out of the pot. Leaving his now prized possession on the step he went down and retrieved Mrs. Pendleton's handkerchief and used it to vigorously mop out the vessel and rinse it one more time before leaving it to collect the water that might keep him alive a few more days.

"Well Ikey, at least you have a pot to piss in and a door to throw it out of." Johnny cackled. Ike found his companion's laughter infectious and before long he was laughing out loud with him.

"I'm losing my mind Johnny, but at least I'm in good company." Ike said, laughing again. "I think I'll go back down for breakfast."

He went back down and finished the biscuits. The bacon was still good but he couldn't force himself to eat the eggs so he threw them out the door. "Well, here goes

Johnny." Ike said, silently this time, and drank out of the chamber pot. As thirsty as he was, the water was delicious.

"You know Ike, we've drank out of worse, ain't we?"

"Yes, Johnny, some of the creeks we've drawn our water from were down stream of some pretty awful things and we survived. We even drank Sarge's coffee and lived. I've got water enough to drink for a while now if I don't drown." Ike mused as he noticed how water was pooling on the floor of the cellar. He heard the clock start to strike again and instinctively counted the chimes, each chime came slower and the sixth strike was more of a thud, the clock had run down.

With his thirst and hunger out of the way for a while Ike began to study the problem of the lock again. The big pistol looked like it might make an excellent hammer if there was an anvil available. He took the remaining cartridges out of the LeMat and laid them on the table. Working himself into an awkward but tolerable position he managed to get the lock onto the stone that supported the lowest step and banged away on it with the handle of the gun. The brass face of the lock bent inwards and the repeated blows loosened the rivets that held it on. Half an hour of hammering opened a gap into which Ike managed to insert the end of the butter knife. The rain had ceased without him noticing as he worked his fingers raw, prying and twisting on the mangled lock until at last he heard a satisfying click. The lock was open!

Ike was about to run shouting up the wet steps when he heard voices in the yard. He froze at the bottom and listened. The murmuring was getting closer. "Well Johnny, looks like I may be out of the frying pan and into the fire." He said, this time internally.

"Cain't be much worse than what you been in Ikey." Johnny replied. "The rebels probably won't shoot a man in a nightshirt."

"I might have a hard time explaining the two dead bodies down there though." Ike said, looking over his shoulder at what he had come to think of as a sepulcher.

Ike looked down and realized how ridiculous he would probably look to whoever it was out there. "You're right Johnny, these might be just the right clothes to surrender in."

"I like the sound of that. You sayin' I'm right I mean."

The voices were coming closer and Ike thought one of them sounded familiar. A few seconds later he shouted "Sarge, is that you?"

"Ike, where are you?" Sarge answered.

"I'm down here in the cellar, I'm coming out."

"Lazarus, come forth!" Sarge chuckled as Ike ascended the steps into sunlight that warmed him to his innermost reaches.

Ike's Sergeant and his companions stood with their mouths open and stared at the specter that emerged from the cellar. The sight of Ike in the damp night shirt with his eye patch and beard left the normally talkative officer speechless.

"It's a long strange tale and I will tell it after I get some real clothes on, I know where there are some that will fit me in the house." Ike said to his flabbergasted audience.

Sarge stepped forward and grinned at Ike "I wanted you to be able to shake my trembling old hand once more before I pass on."

Ike took his Sergeant's hand and shook it with mock solemnity and then took his Father in a bear hug. The two men stood holding each other and shaking with emotion.

"I had given you up for dead until Emma's folks sent me your letter. I think they were mad at first but they were glad to hear that you were alive and figured you had your reasons for sending the letter the way you did. I thought I understood what you were up to with all that rot about unpleasantness and not changing your position. The boys and I used up some of our reenlistment furlough to sneak over here and look for you."

"Are we in Union or Rebel territory?"

"Not quite sure right now, but the Rebs are stretched pretty thin around here and we're not far from our own camps. Why don't you get some clothes on and let's hear the story. Is it all right to go in the house?" Sarge asked.

"The homeowner won't object, she's down there in the cellar, dead."

"Dead! Did you kill her?" Sarge asked.

"No, she had an accident after she killed her brother, he's down there too."

"Merciful God!" Sarge exclaimed.

"Yes indeed." Ike responded, listening to Johnny shouting his "Amen" and laughing with joy.

As Ike was upstairs in Todd's room changing in to his uniform, Johnny was singing a Negro Spiritual with gusto. Ike had to admit that Johnny was in fine voice. "Your singing has improved since the first time I heard it Johnny, the first song I remember you singing was something about a 'young girl from McGrass' and I believe you were way off key." Ike said.

"Well, I always sing when I'm happy, Ikey, and I'm happier than I've ever been and I know there's more on the way. Hey Ikey, that part in the letter about your Pa, with the tremblin' old hands, that was my idea you know. Purty clever of me wasn't it? I'd like to of seen the look on his face when he saw that one!" Johnny said with glee.

"I couldn't figure out why I wrote that Johnny, I couldn't seem to remember that my own Pa was my Sergeant, but my mind was still pretty muddled then. Thank you....for that and for so much more. You saved me from Mrs. Pendleton, and maybe from myself."

"That's alright Ikey, I owed you that and a whole lot more, an' it's what I got to stay here for anyway. I guess my work's done 'cause the Shepherd's come back to get me now that you're free and I'll be a goin' with him purty quick."

"He's here?" Ike asked with a start, looking around.

"He's everywhere, Ikey, we just cain't always see him, but he's callin me to come with him now."

"So I won't be hearing you anymore?" Ike asked.

"Not 'til you cross that creek, Ikey. You gonna' miss me?"

"In some way I guess I will. You know I haven't really managed to completely mourn your death since you took up residence in my head. Yes Johnny, I'm going to miss you. But I'm sure now that I will hear and see you again."

"We'll have lots to chew on when that happens ol' pard." Johnny said. "But for now, I gotta' get goin' and so do you. Drink lotsa' water before you start tellin' yer' story to Sarge. You'll get dry fer sure."

"I sure won't be drinking out of that chamber pot any more. Goodbye Johnny. Give my regards to the rest of the fellows....and Mrs. Pendleton and Marcus.....and Emma."

"I'll do that Ikey." Johnny said. "Well, I better go see my Granny, now that I'm outta' 'perkytory', and you need to go see your Pa."

Ike felt relief with a trace of melancholy that he wouldn't hear Johnny again in his earthly life. He smiled as he went downstairs to join his comrades.

His Father was admiring a painting of Mrs. Pendleton in the study as the younger men were rummaging through the kitchen looking for food. They had found stale biscuits and muscadine jam and were having a fine time gorging themselves.

Sarge jumped as if he had been stung by a bee. He looked around him and saw Ike entering the room. He resumed his study of the painting as if nothing had happened. "She was an attractive lady wasn't she, Ike?" He said.

"Yes, she was at that." Ike said, studying his father. Something about the way he had jumped and then returned his gaze to the painting seemed odd to Ike, but he was too happy just to have him here and be free from his imprisonment to take much note of this peculiar incident.

"What was her name?"

"Micheline Pendleton." Ike answered and began to recount the happenings of the last few months.

Sarge sat down on one of the comfortable chairs in the study and listened to his Son's story. He tried to concentrate on Ike's narrative, but he was distracted by the feeling that someone had pinched him on his backside just as Ike had entered the room. More disturbing than the pinch was the sound of laughter that had filled his head afterwards. The voice sounded familiar.......

Afterword:

I hope you have enjoyed my little tale. Ike and Johnny feel like old friends to me and I hope you might have become fond of them as well.

If you liked this story I hope you will take a chance on me again and check out my other titles on Amazon.

Sergeant Tom's War
Private Sam
Malchus
Stigmata and Other Stories

Made in the USA
Las Vegas, NV
05 January 2022